iceland
sweden
finland
norway
estonia
latvia
lithuania
iceland
united kingdom
holland
germany
poland
belgium
luxembourg
czech republic
france
slovakia
austria
hungary
romania
switzerland
slovenia
croatia
serbia
portugal
andorra
italy
bulgaria
spain
montenegro
macedonia
albania
greece

Christmas Help

TONY SKUR

GREATEST GENERATION
PUBLISHING

Christmas Help copyright ©2013 by Tony Skur

All applicable copyrights and other rights reserved worldwide. No part of this publication may be reproduced, in any form or by any means, for any purpose, without the express, written permission of the author, except by a reviewer, who may quote brief passages in a review, or as provided by the U.S. Copyright Law.

This book is a work of fiction. While some names, places, and events are historically correct, they are used fictiously to develop the storyline and should not be considered historically accurate. Any resemblance of the characters in this book to actual persons, living or dead, is coincidental and beyond the intent of the author.

Book Design by Russell C. Connor and
Dark Filament Publishing Startup
To see your book in print, contact us at
admin@darkfilament.com

Republic P-47 Thunderbolt image
courtesy of Wikipedia

ISBN:
978-1-62890-087-3

First Edition: 2013

Prologue

"*Bartholomew, come here,*" whispered God. The heavens shook, and dark clouds appeared over west Texas for the first time in three years. Thunder rumbled and rolled across a blackened sky from Weatherford to El Paso. A hot, dry wind forced a tumbleweed across Highway 90 west of the general store in Marfa. In the midst of those serving their penance, a bolt of lightning singed Bartholomew's already clipped wings.

"*Lord, I got the message...I'm on the way.*" He prayed that the summons would end up in a reprieve, an assignment or something, anything other than kicking tumbleweed. He let loose a final kick that sent the wild plant bouncing across the parched field, coming to rest against a rusty barbed-wire fence boundary marker. He felt he had endured his time in his personal purgatory for an eternity, but in his heart he knew better. The shape of the cars and the wings of the aircraft that traveled his assigned area had not changed that much during the time between the great wars. He did notice a greater number of military aircraft in the airspace above the great state of Texas and always thought, given another chance, he could pilot them. All one had to do was pull back on the stick and the nose of the aircraft came to you, and when you pushed forward, the aircraft went away from you. What he had forgotten when he was "shining his ass" for that pretty French milk maid, was this rule was in effect even when flying inverted. He had pulled when he should have pushed. But the rules, as he understood them, allowed no second chances for stupidity in flying or for serving out your penance.

As quick as the appearance of the lightning bolt, Bartholomew was transported to a space before God. He had no visual realization of God, rather a sense of force controlled by his Maker. Rather extraordinary, mused Bartholomew as he viewed the splendor of the heavenly court for the second time. Minor changes in the Maker's justiciary were minute. He was surprised he remembered the décor at all given the fact the Lord laid on him a couple of life times of punting the weed across the desert floor. The columns that appeared to be holding up a canopy of exquisite tropical flora were a little too baroque for his taste. He was amazed that the clash of wispy clouds and startling rainbows sliding amongst the fauna prancing among the plants didn't offend the Almighty's tranquility of the universe. He tried to imagine a much softer setting with less distractions and perhaps scented water cascading into a reflection pool surrounded by naked…

"*Bartholomew, pay attention,*" God said in a stage whisper…and on earth San Francisco experienced a relatively minor earthquake. "*You are to replace Jacob as guardian angel for T.C. Thompson, Jr. He's a fighter pilot and Jacob, being the scholar that he has proven to be, is not equipped to handle the devil may care and risk-taking attitudes all these flying warriors possess. You, on the other hand, led a life, short as it was, filled with daring and a complete disregard for life or limb. Perhaps with your guidance, Thompson will live long enough to fulfill my wishes. I do not want Thompson here until after the conflicts on earth are resolved. Take that portion of My power the people on earth call luck and use it as needed to keep him alive. I trust you to use the limited authority with great care and discretion.*"

"Lord, you're giving me a second chance when the rules say…."

"*Bartholomew,*" interrupted God…San Francisco's San Andreas fault opens and closes momentarily…"*It is My rule book. Go, before I have you back kicking tumbleweed in west Texas.*"

"Yes sir."

"*Bartholomew!*" …The Golden Gate bridge swings back and forth, left and right two feet… "*You do not know if I am a sir, a madam, a wisp of moisture or a swirling mass of matter and if you don't get on with your task, you may never know.*"

Chapter 1

"Mayday, mayday, mayday," were the only words Flight Officer Tommy Thompson transmitted before the aircraft's radio went dead.

Bartholomew caught up with Thompson just as his brand new 1941, P-47's, 2800 horsepower engine quit pulling his fighter aircraft through the sky forty miles south of Lake Superior's shore in Wisconsin.

It appears I get to ride my second thunderbolt of the day, Bartholomew mumbled to himself as he sat cross legged on the wing of this Republic Corporation aircraft. Moments before it had been cruising at three hundred miles per hour. He was enjoying the quiet descent through the gray clouds even though the snowflakes made it difficult to visualize what was in front of them. Perhaps, the angel thought, it was time to use a little bit of that luck.

Thompson, on the other hand, had other things on his mind. I better quit looking outside…there's nothing to see except raindrops splattering against the windshield and gray clouds. Concentrate on the gages. Doggone it… the attitude gyro's tumbled. Now the heading indicator is spinning in circles. The only instruments I have left to keep the wings level is the needle and ball. Don't over control. Keep that needle straight up and ball in the center of the race. It's my last resort to control this ten ton glider. I have to keep this falling crowbar right side up. Keep those wings level. Vertigo keeps telling me I'm in a steep right turn. Not so. Believe your instruments gentlemen. That's what the ground school instructor kept harping. Too late to bail out. Damn engine won't restart. I'm in deep trouble.

He thinks he's in trouble. I've been on the job less than five minutes and I'm suppose to keep him alive. Bartholomew plunged his hand into the bag.

Then, a minor miracle occurred. Thompson was out of the clouds, out of the snow showers, out of altitude and out of ideas except one: aim for the smallest trees. This idea prevailed as he entered a sea of snow-dusted green pine tree tops.

Easing back on the stick in a desperate attempt to slow the rate of descent, the wings clipped ten ninety foot tall trees, snapping the frozen sticks. A logging road filled the windscreen. Although the landing gear handle was in the down position, there wasn't time for the wheels to freefall and indicate down-and-locked. The airspeed indicator's needle pointed at 80 miles per hour as the P-47 slammed onto the snow-covered logging trail.

The trees flashed by. Tommy could have sworn the speed increased as the aircraft slid down the road. Snow, mud, trees, and brush all flew by the cockpit. It seemed as if he were sliding faster then he really was. Just when the ride seemed to be over, the road turned ninety degrees but the airplane continued straight ahead and down the hillside.

It wasn't a steep embankment, only 75 feet long. The rocks jutted out of the ground just high enough to rip the left wing off and send the aircraft upside down into a partially frozen creek. Bartholomew was tossed head first into a snow bank. Tommy was held hanging upside down by his seat belt and shoulder harness. Shaking his head cleared the cobwebs from the bump he took when his leather helmet hit the instrument panel. He felt no pain, and all his limbs seemed to be working. He found no holes in his body, no blood, therefore he reasoned, no sweat.

He couldn't take the tension off the seatbelt mechanism because his weight put too much pressure on the release lever. With a great deal of effort, he reached the survival knife taped to his boot. As the knife started to slice the seatbelt, the aircraft shook and rolled. The movement startled him and his eyes left the seat belt…in that moment of panic the blade nicked his finger. Water rushed into the aircraft, but didn't flood the cockpit. Without warning, the plane was right-side up. As he tried to make sense of what was happening, there was this loud noise caused by an enormous man, swinging the biggest ax he had ever seen. He loomed over the wreck, whacking away at the canopy. A chilling sober thought ran through his mind…this nut with the axe is going to lop my head off. The canopy shattered, and the axe blade stopped in mid-swing inches from his face. "You okay, kid?"

Shaken by the experience, Tommy could only nod to this six foot eight inch giant. The black and red checkered shirt he wore could have passed for a billboard for the Purina Company. Four inch wide suspenders looked like spaghetti straps on his broad shoulders. His blonde, wavy hair stuck out from a saw dust covered red stocking cap. It appeared that any attempt to tame his mane had met with failure.

"Good. Let's get out of this creek before I freeze my ass off."

"Excellent idea," he replied as he rushed to deplane. Tommy stood up, unaware that his seat parachute was still strapped to his butt. The heel of his boot caught on a shard of broken canopy, causing a head first tumble into the swift-moving icy water. Struggling to get on his feet, he slipped and fell again into the three foot deep ice cold pool. Picking him up by the collar, his personal Paul Bunyan led him to the far side of the snow-covered creek. A noise from his aircraft revealed three grinning, gray haired men removing a drag line from his aircraft's wing. Tommy surmised that the big son-of-a-bitch really didn't pick up that 21,000 pound aircraft by himself after all. He had help from his logging crew and a huge John Deer tractor.

Chapter 2

The climb up the creek's bank went slow as Tommy kept slipping, sliding and falling. The sheepskin-lined boots he wore were great for keeping his feet warm at high altitude in the airplane but not worth a damn for climbing through the brush and snow. And right now they were filled with cold water. Out of breath and shivering, he arrived at the top of the bank. He spotted a windowless, weather-beaten log cabin. A chattering squirrel sat on the roof next to a tin pipe chimney that was billowing black smoke. A dressed-out deer, snow-covered with one hind quarter missing, hung high from a tri-pod of birch tree trunks, next to the cabin. The cabin looked palatial compared to spending time in the woods under a lean-to made from his parachute. Better yet, it looked warm. Tommy was struggling to make it to the cabin. His feet were cold and his body shivering. He couldn't control his hyperventilating. Trying to keep up with his personal Bunyanesque savior was a chore. The 300 yards to the cabin wore him out.

At the door, the big man looked him over and said, "For a little guy, you go through the woods pretty well. It would have been a hell of lot easier if you had taken off that parachute."

Touching his behind, Tommy confirmed what the big man observed. "Well, my mom always told me to bring a gift when dropping in uninvited. I don't know if you can use it, but it might be good trading material for those creature comforts you might need here in the woods."

Taking the gift, the big man mumbled his thanks. "You know kid, if I cut the parachute into two yard square pieces I bet I could trade them for a little loving. Don't know how many women I can romance because it's too difficult to figure. I do know it's going to be a warm winter." Opening the wooden door, he invited the soaking wet aviator into his north woods home.

Struggling out of his dripping, frozen flying togs, Tommy eased his naked fanny towards the glowing potbelly stove. His six foot, muscular frame was trembling and covered with goose bumps. Bartholomew was hovering there drying his soaked feathers.

"Careful there," cautioned the cabin owner. "If you brush up against that stove you'll be branded with a SEAR'S and ROEBUCKS logo. Dry yourself off with this," throwing a threadbare towel at him.

Stepping back a few inches, Tommy looked over the room. He noticed a kerosene lamp on a table with four straight-back wooden chairs scattered about. Loose, rough sawed wood planks made up the floor. Under a two-door cupboard were a few black and greasy pots, pans, dishes and coffee mugs resting on a saw dust covered shelf. He scanned the cupboard filled with cans of vegetables and coffee grounds. A sack of black beans rested on the edge of the counter. One of the pots sitting on the stove was nearly boiling over. It was filled with black beans and chunks of meat, probably cut from that three-legged deer carcass hanging outside. The aroma made his stomach growl. Another container similar to his grandmother's coffee pot, had some black brew steaming that had a strong fragrance of day old coffee. Tommy grinned in anticipation of putting something warm in his cold body.

Extending his hand, he introduced himself. "My name is Tommy Thompson. Thanks for saving my ass from that freezing water."

A three finger grip engulfed his hand. He tried not to grimace as the curly, blond-headed giant proceeded to mash the living hell out of his hand in friendliness. "I'm Joe Marsh and I didn't pluck you out of that aluminum egg shell by myself. My crew, beat up and old as they are, had the tractor and drag line on your airplane minutes after it splashed into the creek. I haven't seen them move that fast since a moose came after them during the rutting season. I would have bet a month's wages that the moose wanted to make love to them. Take some of those clothes hanging from that peg and cover your body before you catch cold."

Over a steaming cup of coffee, Joe inquired, "Tommy are you okay? Got any broken bones, cuts or bruises. I've got some bandages and iodine if you need them."

"I just need a little tape for my pinkie and thanks for the cup of coffee." His cold hands embraced the warmth given by the cup. He wished he could rub that cup all over his body.

"Well then Tommy, barring a snowstorm, we should be able to get you out of the woods in three days, maybe four days at the most. Me and them three old farts need to extend the logging road another mile. On ordinary acreage we could finish in a day and a half. But the damn snow and the density of the trees are slowing us down. How-some-ever, if you want to help, maybe we could finish faster."

Tommy nodded and in short order found life as a lumber-jack in the north woods a hell of a lot tougher than life as a fighter pilot. Bartholomew's silent giggle sounded much like that bushy tail rodent's chatter up on the roof.

Those days turned out to be the hardest, physical working time in Tommy's life. His job of cutting limbs off fallen trees seemed to be neverending. When one tree was cleansed of branches, tied to the tractor and hauled off, there were shouts of "timber" and another took its place.

On the second day Tommy put on climbing spurs, a safety belt with a saw dangling from the sash. "Are you sure you want to try this, kid? It's not as easy as the movies make it," Joe cautioned.

"Can't be that difficult," he said as he slid down ten feet from his first attempt and landed on his rump. The laughter from the old folks was incentive to try again. Tommy trimmed the branches on the way up the tree. Six feet from the top of the seventy-five foot pine, he removed the undecorated Christmas tree. A shift in his position started the tree to swing in a ten foot arc with Tommy hanging on straining every muscle in his body

"Hey Joe what do I do now?" he screamed.

"If I was you, I'd start down…if you're really scared…pray."

It took ten minutes of trying and three hail Mary's to figure how to slip the safety belt down the tree trunk and stop the fall with his spurs. After four tries he discovered the rhythm and coordination needed in the tree toppers art form.

"Don't try showing off Tommy. Remember all I have to patch you up with is band- aids," Joe shouted to him, stroking his ax five inches into a pine tree trunk.

At the bottom of the tree, Tommy stopped to catch his breath. The crew glanced at him. A sarcastic remarked reached his ears. "If you don't get going up the next tree kid, you'll be here in the woods with us in the spring time."

No sympathy just motivation was his first thought as he threw his safety belt around the next tree. Actually this is kind of fun was his second.

He considered himself to be in good shape, but those four old bastards worked rings around him from sunup to sundown. Every evening after supper of venison stew, he collapsed his aching body on one of the upper bunks of the three beds. The blisters on his hands broke open and hurt almost as much as the muscles in his arms. His pride kept him from complaining. He figured his audience would never let him live it down if he whimpered.

"Hey Tommy," shouted Joe, "join us in this game of black jack. Maybe your luck will change…I don't think it could get much worse."

Tommy groaned and pulled the dusty blanket over his head, shutting out the lantern's yellowish glow, and was asleep in seconds.

Laughing and scratching, those ancient rascals played poker until the wee hours in the morning. As the sun rose, he could tell by the smile on Joe's face that he had been the winner.

True to Joe's estimate, they completed the mile extension in three days. That evening the crew celebrated with the northlands' favorite toddy, snow-shoe grog. This simple concoction of half brandy and half peppermint schnapps was guaranteed to warm body and soul. It also produce a next day headache that rivaled any three day drinking binge hangover.

The three woodsmen shook Tommy's hand, wished him God speed and made him promise to kill a couple of the Hun for them. He half smiled wondering who would be dead first…him or these hard working, hard drinking senior citizens.

The 30-mile trip to the nearest town in what was left of a 1936 Ford ton and a half truck was bone-shaking, nerve-racking, cold. One could say it added up to pure torture to a brain and body suffering the consequences of drinking much too much snow-shoe grog. Tommy was uncomfortable on what was left of the seat, mainly coiled springs. The remainder of the windshield was on the driver's side. The blowing cold air froze the hair in Tommy's nostrils. He felt every bump as the springs pressed hard against his butt. On two occasions the coils took a bite out of his right cheek.

"Any chance of not hitting those pot holes so fast?" His question was ignored as the worn tires spun in the snow. Joe drove indifferent to the dirt road's icy condition. They slid off the trail two times, extending the adventure to town to four hours.

"Have a sip of this grog," Joe insisted. If it weren't for that occasional sip and Joe's infectious laugh as they careened between the trees and occasionally through one, Tommy would have considered the trip a serious threat to life and limb. Bartholomew almost used some of the luck entrusted to him, but thought the jarring ride might be a practical lesson on the virtue of sobriety.

Joe was in a hurry to deposit his guest at the local mom-and-pop grocery store. The truck slid at least ten feet on its bald tires as it came to a halt, billowing black exhaust smoke. "I need to get back to camp real fast," he apologized. "Those three sons of bitches will play black jack for next week's wages, and I need to be in the game. If I don't play and win, I might have to pay someone." That truism almost sobered him up. Joe's farewell to Tommy consisted of a bear hug and a promise of a job after the war because "…for a little fellow, you worked damn hard." Then Joe gave him another bear hug and whispered, "Give 'em hell. I'll be praying for you."

    The grocery store was in a town of 1500 people, only 50 miles from the Volk Army airfield. Tommy noticed the wooden sign hanging on the door had "John and Mary Hanover, Owners" burned on to it. Opening the door to the store triggered three brass bells that announced a visitor's entrance. Whatever was cooking filled the air with the sweet smell of cinnamon and apples. Tommy made his way through the aisles towards the cash register guarded by John and Mary Hanover. He glanced at a two-day-old newspaper laying on a pickle barrel and was surprised to see his own smiling face, complete with leather helmet, goggles and white scarf wrapped around his neck on the front page. Now there's a tiger's portrait, he thought. Stopping to read the article, it stated, "T.C. Thompson, Jr., missing, feared dead. The War Department has notified the president of Thompson Industries that his son is overdue from a routine gunnery mission and that a search is underway." The senior Thompson expressed surprise at the announcemnt and stated "he hadn't heard from his son in over a year." The fact they had not had a loving father/son relationship for the last eight years suddenly became more painful and this bitter truth was his alone to bear. Tommy put the paper down and for a second thought he should call his father. No. Let the government tell him for the last year he had been in training to be a fighter pilot. They're the ones that blew the whistle on me.

Chapter 3

It was Tommy's first and last deer hunting trip with dear old dad or with any one else for that matter. He was eleven years old and still wringing the pain out of his heart after his mother's death in a swimming accident that summer. The memory was anchored in his mind.

"Son, let's go down to the company's rifle range. I bought you this single shot Remington thirty ought six and today you'll get to know how to sight and shoot it." They spent several hours each week together as his father taught him the correct way to hold, load, sight and squeeze the trigger.

"Tommy this is not a toy," his father warned him. "Do not point it at another person and always consider it loaded and ready to fire even though you could swear it's not." He taught his son the way the Marines taught him during World War One, even using some of the same-four letter words.

"Damn it son, keep that fucking weapon pointed down range." Grabbing his son and turning him in the right direction, he shouted, "Your target is that way. Line up the rear and front sight. Keep that bull's eye on the top of that sight picture. Now gently squeeze the trigger. Good shot."

Tommy's time at the range proved worthwhile. He was filled with pride when his dad patted him on his back a week later and remarked, "Son, you're an excellent marksman."

Tommy was really excited that November Saturday morning as his father shook him awake and said, "Rise and shine. Get your rifle, you're going hunting with us." The hunting group of mostly relatives met at five in the morning for a breakfast consisting of roast beef, mashed potatoes and gravy. Hot rolls dripping with butter sopped up whatever gravy was left. Tommy tried hard to conceal how excited he felt. He could only pick at the food on his plate.

The family members left Tommy and his dad in an area that on previous hunts had produce an occasional shot at a deer. And so they sat, father and son, shoulder to shoulder, freezing their asses in that cedar grove. An occasional sip of brandy from his flask kept the chill off the senior Thompson's bones. Those occasions became more frequent as daylight crept into the woods. Tommy was so hyper that he did not need any thing to keep warm. The air was still and the fragrance from the rotting wood heightened Tommy's awareness of the beauty of nature. Out of the corner of his eye, Tommy spotted a movement, and magically, out of nowhere, a doe ambled into the clearing, looking, grazing, then looking some more.

"Dad," he softly whispered…nudging his dozing father, who put his finger to his lips and shook his head. Tommy understood not to shoot the doe. This was his first sighting, and the graceful movement and beautiful lines of the animal amazed him. His heart beat rapidly.

It was less than a minute later when a twelve point buck stepped into the clearing. Satisfied that all was well, the buck grazed as the doe kept watch and then he acted as the lookout while the doe grazed.

The father poked his son, nodded and Tommy put his sights on the buck's lower neck. It was a magnificent picture. The buck's steaming breath blowing from his nostrils, his hoof pawing at the snow trying to uncover blades of grass. His father gave him a hard nudge, but Tommy couldn't pull the trigger. The deer started to walk away as his father ripped the rifle from his hands, took quick aim and dropped the buck. Reloading as he walked forward, he put another round in the deer's neck as the deer turned to peer at the gunman approaching. Tommy remained stationary with tears streaming down his cheeks.

"Cut that crying you wimp," commanded his dad. Try as he might to stifle his sobs, he couldn't, and his dad slapped him hard. "Stop it, damn it, stop it!" he was yelling at him. Cuffing him, pushing him towards the fallen deer until Tommy fell on the deer forcing blood to ooze from the deer's mouth. Tommy puked all over his dad's trophy deer. His dad never let him forget that day. His dad told the story at every family gathering, making the event more hilarious every time.

There were no father and son moments to remember. Tommy recalled, he never hugged me or played catch with me. Not once did he show up at the baseball games I starred in. And never invited me to hunt with him again. Just as well, Tommy thought, I would have told him to go fuck himself.

Chapter 4

John and Mary Hanover were a pleasant-looking couple in their late forties, standing at the cash register next to a double-barrel 12-gauge shot gun. Tommy's four-day growth of peach fuzz, filthy clothes that reeked of burnt pine wood and sweat, along with his dirt-caked hands did little to convince the Hanovers that this stranger was a cash customer. Flashing his best smile and extending his grimy hand, he said, "I'm Flight Officer T.C. Thompson. May I use your phone? I'll reverse the charges." The Hanovers listened to him explain to the captain on the other end of the phone line where he was and what had cause him to crash.

"We've been looking too far north for you, Thompson. The lousy weather hasn't helped our efforts. Don't exert yourself, you might have internal injuries. An ambulance should be there in an hour or so," the captain instructed. After all the hard work Tommy had done in Joe's logging camp, he did his best not to laugh until he hung up the phone.

Mary and John were doing their best to not act surprised that the young man whose face graced the county's newspaper was standing in front of them eating a Baby Ruth candy bar as nonchalant as a school boy. The phone's ringing interrupted their evaluation of this ragged looking aviator.

"Mr. Thompson, the rescue will be delayed as the roads are closed due to the snow storm. Please find a place to lie down. You may have internal injuries. I apologize for the delay. Don't give up hope and stay put," the captain ordered.

"Yes sir," Tommy promised. Where in the hell did he think I was going?

"Would you mind if I stay here and await my so called rescue team," Tommy half snickered.

Mary looked him over with a jaundiced eye and noted, "Under all that smoke and dirt, you're just a kid."

"Ma'am, I'm almost nineteen, a fighter pilot, and this war between our country, the Axis and the Japanese takes me out of the kid category," he boasted.

"Well, Mr. Fighter Pilot, there's a bathtub in the house back there, and you can use it. I mean, you can really use it to soak that mess off your body. Throw those clothes out to John, and I'll clean them the best I can," Mary urged. "And clean the tub when your finished."

"John, get him some of your work clothes. The size is close enough." It was obvious to Tommy that Mary cracked the whip around this household.

John led him to the bathroom, showed him where the towels and a razor were kept and left. He returned in short order with a shirt, sweater, slacks, socks and a water glass full of red wine. "Takes a man to do what you're doing, Tommy, but Mary will never understand that flying and fighting a war is not all fun and games. Bathe at your leisure as the roads to the airfield are under three feet of snow with drifts as high as rooftops. I'll be surprised if they can get through tomorrow, much less tonight." Bartholomew nodded his agreement and tried to get that burnt pine smell out of his tattered wings.

The soaking in hot water in the deep bathtub with bear claw legs, the wine, and the quiet were just too comforting to Tommy. After he shaved and dressed he sat on the bed to put on John's socks. He felt the need to rest and put his head on a down filled pillow. Thirty seconds later he was sound asleep.

John and Mary went to check on him thinking he had drowned. Mary took a quilt from the closet and covered Tommy with the gentleness of a mother.

As they left the room, she turned to John and whispered ,"Scrubbed up, that boy warrior isn't half bad looking." To herself she mused that in his uniform of pinks and greens, with those leg spreaders, a term she learned from her mother that meant aviator wings, on his chest, he'd be damn hard to say no to.

Chapter 5

Tommy woke with a feeling that things weren't right. His eyes focused first on the business end of a double-barrel, 12-gauge shotgun that was two inches from his nose. As he straightened his crossed eyes to look up the barrels, he focused on a set of eyes that were as metallic in their grayness as the gun barrels. He wasn't sure, but the rest of the face looked a lot like a younger version of Mary Hanover. Her auburn hair was almost covered with a stocking cap, her cheeks were tinted with a blush, and her eyes looked menacing, in a cute sort of way. Her heavy wool sweater couldn't disguise the figure of a blossoming young woman, who at this moment, appeared mean as hell.

"What have you done with my parents? What are you doing in my dad's clothes? What are you doing in their bed? Answer me asshole!" She wasn't screaming, but there was no doubt in his mind as to who was in control.

Without blinking and ever so slowly, Tommy tried to explain, "Your parents let me in to wash up, gave me the clothes, I guess I fell asleep. If they are not here, I don't know where they are…and could you back off a little…"

"Get out of that bed and march your ass to the phone. Don't get smart or I'll shoot you," she interrupted in a sharp, fear filled cry.

He was quick to comply and finally found the nerve to ask, "Are you related to John and Mary?"

"Shut up," she commanded.

At the phone she was surprised to find a note taped to the wooden crank box. "Read it," she demanded, raising the shot gun towards the note.

Clearing his throat he read, "Peggy, I knew you couldn't pass up the phone without using it. There's a young man asleep on our bed. A boy fighter pilot that crashed in the bush three days ago. Try to be quiet. We are at the wedding reception for the Byrnes. Come on over. If Tommy's awake, bring him. Mom."

Silence.

"Peggy, I would be honored to escort you to that reception, even if you didn't have that shotgun pointed at me," a grinning T.C. Thompson, Jr., announced.

Chapter 6

Peggy and Tommy walked the three blocks to the Byrnes' wedding reception almost in complete silence. Silver dollar size snowflakes floated by a gentle wind fell in the black night. Peggy blinked as one caught her long eye lashes and cart-wheeled across her face. She stumbled but did not fall because Tommy, already at her elbow, moved in close and caught her by her arm. She turned as if they were dancing. With her face inches from his she said, "Thanks." He held her close just long enough to breathe in the scent of roses faintly mixed with the arctic air.

"I think I could I could get used to holding you like this," Tommy sighed. She let him hold her for a brief moment. Then with great reluctance pulled away. They continued their walk to the reception. She did, however, let him hold on to her hand.

"Thanks" was the first word she had spoken since he had read her mother's note. "Damn it," she said, "I'm not embarrassed by holding that shot gun on you Tommy. I was frightened out of my mind, and raced to a conclusion that could have ended in disaster. When I entered the house and no one answered my greeting, I went to my parents' bedroom and was startled to see you in their bed. My fear for my parents' safety was too much for me and I went to get the shotgun…which, given the same circumstances, I would do again."

In her heart of hearts she was certainly glad he wasn't a robber or murderer or both because he was such a good-looking rascal. There was something about him that was electrifying and caused goose bumps on her neck the second she held his hand. She thought that this stranger was worth holding on to.

At the reception held in the church's basement, Tommy never left her side for more than a minute. He talked about everything and nothing. "How old are you and what subjects do you like in school?"

"I'm almost eighteen and I love all my subjects," she declared. It wouldn't have mattered to Tommy if she said she was thirty five and hated every minute she was in school.

"Do you ice skate, Tommy? After the reception we could help the other kids clear the pond if you want to. We could borrow dad's skates for you."

"Actually I'm pretty good on ice…let's do it," was his quick reply.

He just wanted to hold her…on the dance floor or ice skating rink, he didn't care where…and look in to those shiny metallic gray eyes. They danced all evening, sometimes too close. When the last notes of 'Good Night Ladies' sounded they rushed to get their skates.

During the four-piece band's breaks, Mary would grab Tommy's arm and whisk him off to introduce him to all her friends. "This is a lost fighter pilot whom I'm hosting for the next couple days." Mary's face reflected a hint of pride while her firm grip on his arm kept him in her family's circle. The townspeople made the connection with the newspaper article and were nice enough to not make a big deal out of Tommy's crash… it was as if airplanes fell out of the sky with regularity near their town. Mary released him to her daughter's custody after the band's break as the first note escaped from the accordion. When they whirled away, someone remarked that they made a nice looking couple. "Nonsense," Mary said, but she smiled like a Cheshire cat. When they left to go skating, she grabbed John and said, "Let's go make some hot chocolate for that group of skaters." In her mind she wanted to make sure that skating was all that was going on at that pond at the town's Memorial Park.

They arrive as Tommy was falling backwards holding on to Peggy's arm. She landed on top of him. "So you're pretty good on ice…ha." He pulled her back down as she tried to get up. Laughing together, their faces inches apart, she stopped and kissed him. Breaking away, she said ,"You really are pretty good on ice."

"Okay you two… time for some hot chocolate to cool you off," mother Mary proclaimed. Brushing themselves off, they skated hand in hand towards her parents. John looked at Mary and whispered, "She's too young. Hell, they're both too young."

Turning to John, Mary replied, "That was only a kiss and we instilled a pretty good set of values in that girl. Let's not ruin a fun evening by over blowing an innocent moment."

"Alright but remember you're the one who said he'd be tough to say no to."

The military ambulance arrived two days later, and the medics insisted that Tommy lie down on the gurney for the trip back to the base even after he greeted them at the door standing on two good legs, holding three cases of beer stacked one on top of the other.

"I hope you two corpsmen have time for a cup of coffee and some of my cinnamon rolls," Mary asked.

It was an invitation no GI could resist. "We always have time for coffee and we'll make time for the cinnamon rolls, ma'am," answered the tall skinny sergeant. "Private Williams, put that beer in the ice box for this lady. Mr. Thompson join us at the table and we'll see how beat up you really are. Williams, when you finish, join us."

An hour later Tommy was laughing as they loaded him into the ambulance because both corpsmen had a cinnamon roll clenched between their teeth as the lifted the gurney on board.

"Thanks Mrs. Hanover," yelled Private Williams as they drove off. "

"Tell Peggy I'll call her tonight," Tommy shouted as the door slammed shut.

After his return to the base, he was released from the hospital by the flight surgeon once he passed a complete physical. When he told the doctor of his time as a lumberjack after the crash and his ice skating with Peggy after her school day the doctor just shook his head. "Mr. Thompson, get the hell out of my office… you're wasting my time."

He met with an accident board that reviewed the maintenance report on the engine's internal failure. The report stated the loss of engine oil through a metal oil line worn through from chaffing against a bulk head caused the engine to seize. They found no pilot error in any of his actions. They recommended Flight Officer Thompson to continue the advance gunnery training program operating out of the airfield.

Whenever he had a day off or even a few free hours in the evening, he would drop by to see Peggy. She was a senior in high school, class of 1944, and a virgin.

One night as they wandered around town, Tommy turned her towards him. "Peggy, you know how I feel about you. We've been seeing each other for a month and I think you want me as much as I want you. When you press your body close to mine I can feel you shudder. Let me…"

"No! Don't do this to me, Tommy. It will mean so much more if we wait. I'll wait for you because I think I'm in love with you."

And when she kissed him goodbye six weeks later, she was still a senior in high school and still a virgin.

She maintained this status in spite of Tommy's efforts to the contrary. During those passionate, frustrating sessions together, she kept thinking, if great hands make a pilot, he must be damn good at moving that airplane across the sky. She didn't want to lose him, but she didn't want to sacrifice something that could only be given once. If marriage ever crossed Tommy's mind, he sure hadn't mentioned it.

What crossed Tommy's mind was the fact that when he was asleep his dreams of her were so real that when he reached out for her he would fall out of bed. He wasn't sure what these dreams meant, except maybe it wasn't just lust he felt for her…maybe it was really love. If this were love, he sure was confused.

Chapter 7

Peggy walked across the stage on June 6, 1944, to give her valedictorian speech. Earlier that day the radio announced the Allied invasion of France. Tears were streaming down her cheeks and her hands trembled. "Please," she begged the audience through quivering lips, "pray with me for our troops that are storming the beaches." Her voice trembled as she pleaded, "Pray for their safety and for a victorious end to this war." As the audience knelt and said their silent prayers, Flight Officer Thompson was raking the enemy lines with rockets and 50 caliber bullets from his P-47's eight machine guns mounted in the aircraft's wings.

Flying from Royal Air Force Base Ibsley, England, he flew three sorties that day. Flying low through the early morning gray sky, Tommy and 150 fighter pilots in their heavily laden P-47's, targeted pillboxes, machine gun emplacements and the Panzer tanks that pinned the American troops on the beaches at Normandy. Overhead hundreds of

B-17 and B-24 bombers were attacking the German forces trying to reach the shores of the English Channel. Between them, C-47's filled with 101st Airborne Divisions' Screaming Eagle paratroopers headed north for their drop. The English Channel was filled with hundreds of ships. The skies were filled with hundreds of fighters, bombers and transport aircraft struggling to stay in their assigned block of airspace. All this effort to support the Allied invasion ground force. Still the shore line was tinted red from the blood of hundreds of fallen infantry and sailors.

After the first sortie, Tommy's crew chief ask," Sir, are we doing any good?"

Remembering the bodies washing up on shore, Tommy hesitated then shook his head. "We're stalled on the beaches. Hurry up and get me refueled and re-armed. They need us."

Fifteen minutes later he and the flight of four were airborne, determined to make a difference in the battle. The fighter group's losses were significant as they pressed the attack on ground targets. Shouts of "look out... pull up" came too late for the pilots whose eyes were fixated on a ground target collided with each other. The sounds from those collisions were lost in the deafening rumble of explosions caused by the fifteen inch shells landing on the enemy fortifications. Tommy's head moved as if on a swivel. Kicking in left rudder and violently pushing forward on his stick, he kept his aircraft clear of two fighters that collided canopy to canopy. The resulting fire ball enveloped his aircraft for an instant. The heat and burning oil smell was fleeting. The event was captured in his memory as a still photograph and was filed deep in some album of his brain forever. The excessive chatter on a crackling static filled radio frequencies, coupled with the intense air activity and anti-aircraft fire made it impossible for flight leaders to figure out which aircrew was lost.

On the ramp after the second mission, Tommy looked at his crew chief and answered the unasked question, "We're still on the beach. Let me help with the refueling."

"No sir. We have men stumbling over each other wanting to help. Grab a cup of coffee and a donut. We'll be finished after we patch a couple holes."

"Forget the patches. I'll take her as she is."

"It's your ass, sir."

And I'll make sure it stays in one piece, Bartholomew asserted as he kicked the tire.

Tommy led White flight of three P-47's on this last sortie. Each aircraft had three five hundred pound bombs, two on the wings and on under the fuselage. The flight was diverted off the beach to destroy a truck convoy.

"Hey Tommy, do you see what I see?"

"Damn it, use the call sign. There are four guys named Tommy in the group."

"Don't get your skivvies in a knot. White one check ten o'clock low."

"White flight, arm 'em up. There's ten trucks plus two tanks. Lead's in."

Eight of the nine bombs hit their intended targets taking out seven trucks and one tank. The last bomb was still on the centerline as the plane impacted the ground in front of the second tank sending a ball of flame over the Panzer cremating everyone within a one hundred foot radius.

Tommy's yell of, "White three pull up" fell on dead ears as a golden bullet had pierced the pilot's heart. His voice filled with anger, he shouted the order, "Join up, White two." White leader rolled his aircraft over into a shallow dive and expended every fifty caliber bullet he carried into the string of burning wreckage.

His crew chief knew better than to ask. There were too many holes to ignore and Tommy's face was red and the vein on his forehead pulsated. He had never lost a wingman and this weighed heavily on his injured pride. "Isn't she ready to go yet chief?" he demanded

"No sir, she's not."

Tommy was ready to explode as he stepped closer to the crew chief. From behind him a hand reached out to his shoulder and pulled him around. "Mr. Thompson, that plane's not ready. There's too much battle damage. Go to debriefing."

"But Colonel…"

"That's an order Mr. Thompson! The war will still be going tomorrow, and the next day and more than likely the day after that. Go on son, get the hell out of here."

Shoulders hunched forward, Tommy left for debriefing as the Colonel told the crew chief, "Have it ready for tomorrow. That caged tiger is ready to pounce and lay some hurt on the enemy…real or imagined."

Tommy was credited with destroying two pillboxes and one Panzer tank that sixth day of June. He also picked up a reputation as a "magnet ass." It appeared that every bullet fired from a German infantryman's rifle was drawn to Tommy's aircraft.

During the next two weeks the group's mission was to continue interdiction of the Germans' supply structure and support allied troops in contact with the enemy.

"For Christ's sake Mr. Thompson, can't you dodge any better than what your doing. I've patched up the tail feathers on this Jug so often, they look like Heddy Lamar's polka dot sarong."

"Sarge, I'm thankful they haven't learned to lead a target correctly otherwise it would be my ass that was polka dotted. Besides, this extra work keeps you out of the bar, out of fights and keeps those stripes on your arm. So let's both be thankful to whoever is watching over us."

"*You're welcome,*" Bartholomew sighed.

His crew chief never did run out of aluminum to patch up the holes in his airplane that Tommy kept bringing back to him. However his aggressiveness in delivering ordinance at tree top level brought complaints from the maintenance officer to the squadron commander. Several one on one sessions between Tommy and his commander had little, if any, effect on his method of supporting allied troops in contact with enemy forces.

"Damn it Thompson is your eyesight that bad that you feel you have to run over the enemy?"

"Well sir…"

"Don't give me any excuses, just straighten up and fly right. And if I hear any rumors that your crew chief is going to put a bayonet on your pitot tube I'm going to ground your ass. Get out of here I've got more important things to do other than trying to keep you alive."

That's my job and a very difficult job it is, Bartholomew thought.

In mid June, the fighter group moved to Deux Jumeuax, France, and continued fighter sweeps throughout western France and Belgium.

* * *

Peggy's summer was bittersweet. Tommy's absence tugged at her heart as she waited for Tommy's infrequent letters.

"Peggy, you received a letter this morning…"

"Is it from Tommy, mom?"

"No, it's from the university. Careful honey, don't rip the envelope to pieces, it might contain some important news."

"Oh mom" she sang out, "the University of Wisconsin not only accepted me but is giving me a four year scholarship in the School of Business." She whirled, filled with joy, around the kitchen on her bobby sox covered feet.

"Peggy, that business school is a male domain where women aren't likely to succeed," Mary cautioned.

"Well I will," Peggy declared, hands on her hips. "No amount of pressure from friends, relatives or faculty is going to change my mind."

Throughout the summer, Tommy's letters to Peggy were infrequent and contained no information as to where he was stationed or what he was doing. The censors had not chewed up his letters for Tommy wrote only of the fun times they had when they were together.

In early September, as she registered for college, Tommy was flying on the wing of his flight commander, Lieutenant O'Brian over war torn France. American troops were pinned down behind a hedgerow by German infantry.

"Lead, could you vary the attack heading. I'm taking hits," requested an excited wingman through a radio frequency filled with electrical interference.

"Green two, shut up and follow me!"

"Roger wilco," snapped Tommy. A not so Christian thought rambled through his mind…thanks a lot you son of a bitch.

Following his leader as they rolled in again on the same heading for the fifth time, the air turned black as the flack surrounded both aircraft. "Green one, my engine oil pressure is zero and …oh shit…the engine quit. I'm too low to bail out," Tommy cried out in a near soprano voice as shrapnel sliced his aircraft.

Before a terrified Lieutenant O'Brian could answer he and his P-47 exploded into a thousand pieces.

Tommy busily dodged the larger remnants of his leader's aircraft and glided away from the enemy as he said to himself, "Thank God the field is fairly flat." Looking through an oil smeared windshield he tried to use aileron and rudders to turn his flaming aircraft away from the hedgerow he was sliding into, but to no avail. The heat became unbearable as the hedgerow started to burn and Tommy's eyebrows were singed as he leaped from the cockpit and sprinted to what he hoped was safety.

"Welcome to our part of hell," a mud covered U.S army private called as he tackled Tommy and pulled him down. Machine gun bullets whistled over their heads.

"Thanks a lot buddy. I think we should move away from the aircraft before it explodes," an energized Tommy suggested.

"Sounds like a good idea to me. Keep your ass low as we crawl out of this… the natives are not friendly," advised his teenage guide. "On the other side of this hedgerow our troops are mobilizing for a strike against that enemy group you and that other aircraft were pounding. Why in the hell did you guys make all your attacks from the same direction? Do you pilots have a death wish or something?"

"No death wish, it's just some of us have a steel trap mind when it comes to tactics," a subdued Tommy commented. He remembered his last unkind thought about his flight leader and for a fleeting moment almost felt ashamed of himself.

Christmas Help

"No second chances for stupidity in the air," Bartholomew said as he greeted a bewildered O'Brian as the lieutenant pulled himself together.

"You won't be much use to us as we move forward, " an unshaven sergeant remarked, splattering Tommy's burned face with some water from his canteen. "You can help the medic move the wounded closer to the road. There should be a truck or two here in the next couple hours to transport them to an aid station. Thanks for softening up the krauts. Okay men, lock and load. Start firing as you clear the hedge. Follow me and for Christ sake don't shoot me in the ass."

The next day, riding back to his squadron in the back of a four by four truck carrying a dozen walking wounded, including the kid who helped him through the hedgerow, Tommy wrote to Peggy;

"Sometimes there really aren't enough hours in the day or days in your life to do all the things you want to do or just to try…maybe even try just once. If you want to major in business, then ignore all those who say that's not your place because you're a woman. Do it because you're you, because it is your time, and your life. Do it because we have no guarantee on how much time we have to use." And then perhaps an afterthought, he scribbled, "Marry me, and I'll love you for all the time we have left."

She wrote back immediately on the flimsy, tissue thin, pale blue "V" mail paper; "There is time for us. There's time to love and a time to hold and comfort each other. And the first time we're together again, I'll marry you."

That time came sooner than either one expected. In mid October he was shot down by ground fire for the second time. He suffered some nasty cuts and an infected bullet wound that required stitches as a result of that action. He was rescued and returned to his base by the British infantry.

Tommy's commander was about to lift his nightly glass of Wild Turkey as the flight surgeon sat down next to him. "Have one on me, Doc."

"Must be a big favor about to be unloaded on me, and yes I will. Gin, straight up bartender."

"Thompson's been a real magnet ass as of late and nothing I have said seems to temper his aggressiveness. Are his wounds sufficient enough to keep him on the ground for a while?"

"How long's a while?"

"Say thirty days."

"If you're asking for thirty days convalescent leave I have no problem with that. Anything else I should know about this kid before I say yes?"

"I received a British infantry officer's written communication stating he has recommended Tommy for the award of the Military Cross for gallantry during an active ground operation against the enemy. I can't believe one of my aviators is getting a sparkly for engaging the enemy on the ground. I don't have all the particulars but I'm convinced that this kid needs some time away from the air war."

"In that case I'll have the orders cut tomorrow." Lifting his glass, "Here's to our teenage hero and all the other lads holding their own against the enemy."

* * *

Tommy was able to catch a ride to London on a twin engine C-47, known with great affection through out the Air Corps as the "gooney bird". As he limped up to the counter at the London base operations, a white-haired, military contract international airline captain was telling the clerk, "I have room for one more military passenger if you could get him to the flight line in the next minute or two."

Tommy interrupted and asked, " Sir, do I qualify?"

The captain glanced at Tommy's single row of ribbons indicating the Air Medal, Distinguish Flying Cross and Purple Heart and said, "Son, you're overqualified." Twenty four hours and three shorter airplane hops later, Tommy was standing ankle deep in snow outside the gate at Truax Field, Madison, Wisconsin with his thumb in the air.

"Hitchhiking is not exactly what a flight officer is expected to do, but what the hell," Tommy muttered to himself, "what more can they do to me…I already have orders to go back to war."

Chapter 8

The pale green Chevy slid ten feet past Tommy. The horn honked and a gloved hand waved Tommy inside. He was picked up by a gray haired gentleman whose car interior smelled like old pipe tobacco. "Where are you headed soldier?" the old gent asked, his unlit pipe clenched firmly in his stained teeth.

"I'm heading to Prairie View," replied Tommy as he rubbed his hands to warm them up.

"Why, that's in the middle of nowhere, son. You sure won't find too many girls to party with in that neck of the woods," the wrinkle face said with a grin.

"I don't need the party types anymore. I'm going to marry the prettiest girl in the state. I have twenty nine more days left before I go back to France, and I don't want to waste any one of them."

"You been there and you're going back? Hell, I thought you were one of those canteen cowboys who expect the girls to swoon because they're wearing a uniform. Son,

I'll have you there in three hours barring any blizzard. My name's Horatio, what's yours?"

"I'm Tommy, and sir you don't have to go out of your way."

The Chevrolet moved forward, spinning it's wheels on the packed snow. "Tommy, you're the first fighting soldier that I've met. I sure as hell ain't going to put you out in the snow. Did you kill any of those Nazi bastards?"

Tommy hesitated…this is going to be a long ride, but, then again, it's warm in here. If I don't tell him something, this old man is going to pepper me with questions for the next three hours. And what the hell, maybe if I verbalize my nightmare, possibly I'll forget it. And for the first and last time, Tommy decided to tell about being shot down the second time.

"Yes sir I did," he answered.

"Would you tell me about it?" the salt and peppered hair driver asked.

"Look mister, I don't mind telling you because that action is all tied up inside me. Maybe telling you will make me sleep better."

"Was it that bad, Tommy?"

"It didn't start any different from most missions and I sure didn't expect anything unusual to happen. My flight leader and I were supporting British troops on the ground south of Cana, France. 'Support for troops in contact' our brass called it."

"I guess the brass can come up with justification for a mission at the drop of a hat," Horatio interjected.

"In this instance they really were justified. The weather had been lousy for three days and this was our first opportunity to engage the enemy in this sector. The British troops were pinned down by some elements of a panzer division that included two tanks that were well dug in… making it difficult, if not impossible, to hit and destroy them with our five hundred pounders."

"Seems to me that you air corps pilots should have been able to neutralize them?"

"Ordinarily we should have but our attack options were limited because the opposing parallel lines looked to be separated by only two hundred, maybe three hundred yards. Our options for attacking were limited, and we ended up making each pass on the same heading, which solved the tracking problem for the German gunners."

"As an old pheasant hunter, I can appreciate the benefit of not having to guess where the birds are going to come from," suggested the experienced fowl seeker.

"Right you are," answered Tommy. "When they figured out that my leader and I were going to be as regular as the train from Munich to Frankfurt, it only took four passes for them to solve the lead portion of the firing equation, and that is when they knocked me out of the sky."

"Did you bail out?" Horatio asked anxiously.

"No, I was too low. I came down fast between the two lines. Unfortunately, the airplane bounced fifteen feet and yawed violently before the left wing tip dug into the ground. More unfortunately, my death grip on the stick held the trigger down and I sprayed fifty caliber bullets over both the good and bad guys lines."

"Holy cow shit," exclaimed the excited listener. "Were you hurt?"

"Well the airplane did slide like it was on manure but I was strapped in tight and didn't get a scratch."

"What luck," the fascinated hearer blurted out.

"You bet your wrinkled buns it was, and I think I deserve a little credit for that save," Bartholomew mumbled.

"When the aircraft stopped sliding, I ran towards our lines but damn if they didn't started shooting at me. Thinking I was disoriented, I turned and ran towards the other line, but those sons of bitches start shooting at me. One bullet hit my calf as I ran up an incline and dove head first into a deep crater. My landing was cushioned by three bodies lying there…one German and two British infantrymen."

"Your luck seemed to have run out when that bullet hit your leg," Horatio commented.

"*Never*," shouted Bartholomew as the car hit a patch of ice and momentarily went side ways for fifty feet, and then straightened out down the center of the road.

"Your luck seems to be working well tonight," chuckled Tommy.

There was a couple minutes of silence as Horatio settled down before he asked, "What happened in the crater and didn't your wound hurt?"

"I untangled myself from my hosts and checked the small hole in my leg. The wound stung at first but after I used my scarf as a tourniquet both the pain and the blood stopped. I looked over the bodies and noted that one of the Brits had his throat sliced open. The other had a bayonet sticking in his chest, his service revolver still in his hand ready to take on any German ghost sniper that might be lurking in the shadows. The Kraut had a single wound, a neat hole in his forehead, but very little remained of his head from his ears back. Binoculars hung from his neck and his MP 40 machine gun was at his side. You know it didn't smell too good in that hole."

"Weren't you scared?"

"You bet I was…and a little nauseous from the unpleasant odor from the boated bodies, but the need for self preservation took over. I gathered up the equipment from the slain warriors for my war of survival. My weapons inventory consisted of the Brit's service revolver, the Kraut's binoculars and MP40 machine gun, and best of all there were two sniper rifles resting on the lip of the crater, each pointing at one of the lines."

"You prepared yourself well. Did you sit back and wait for the enemy to attack you?"

"No sir, I got my balls up and peered over the side of the crater. My position gave me a superior advantage to look over both lines. Also, I could see where both German tanks were dug in. They were entrenched so deep in the ground, it would take a direct hit from a 1000 pound bomb to render them useless. The crater I had jumped into must have been the observation point for both sides, and the contest for this prize had so far ended in a draw."

"Then you slipped down deep in the crater and awaited your fate, right?"

"No, like the dummy I am, I watched as both sides used my disabled aircraft for target practice. Within minutes, there was a puff of smoke from one of the wings and then the aircraft burst into flames. Small explosions erupted and thick black smoke drifted skyward. Both sides gave a loud cheer claiming victory over the twit that had inadvertently hosed them."

"And you were that twit," laughed his chauffer.

"Yes sir I was, but I took advantage of the noise from the explosions to fire a trial shot with the British sniper rifle on what was left of the tail of my aircraft. The sight was right on the money at almost a hundred yards," explained Tommy.

"Don't tell me you went after the enemy," a wide eyed car driver said in disbelief.

"It wasn't like I was charging them. More like using my position and training to inflict a little damage on the ones who shot me down."

"Revenge?" ventured Horatio.

"No, more like payback. I sighted down towards the tanks but there wasn't a target available as the men bent over to move munitions from one area to the next. I moved the sight picture down the line and stopped on a pair of eyes squinting through binoculars at the wreckage. I squeezed off a round and watched the man slump over as the bullet hit inches low but in his neck.'

"How far away was he?"

"About 150 yards."

"Pretty good shooting, Tommy. Where did you pick up that skill?"

"From my father and endless practice with the army. I qualified "Expert" with the Garand M1 rifle."

"I bet you thought you were an angel of death."

"No, the feeling was more like a kid at the carnival shooting gallery...only no kewpie dolls for prizes. There was movement near the closest tank as an ammunition can was being passed up to a man in the turret. I was able to hit first the man reaching down out of the hatch and then the man reaching up. I could see another man who appeared to be yelling and pointing towards my position. It took two shots from my sniper rifle, and he fell silent. Then all hell broke loose!"

"Meaning what?" an anxious Horatio inquired.

"Meaning the two tanks' turrets moved, pointing in my direction, and I dove for the bottom of the crater. The left flank of men and the two tanks opened up on my position. I desperately tried to claw myself deeper as the 88-millimeter shells hit the sides of the mound. I counted two earth-shaking impacts before the dirt, the bodies of those already dead and blackness covered me. When I awoke, the silence was broken only by the ringing in my ears. I finally convinced myself to peer over the edge to see if any of the Germans were coming to take back the vantage spot. To my amazement, there weren't any of the enemy coming up the hill. Not a soldier nor a tank. They were gone."

"I give up, where did they go?" asked Horatio.

"Damned if I know. I was in a state of euphoria until I heard a round slam into a rifle's receiver directly behind me."

"Nazis?"

"No, a voice with a thick cockney accent yelled something in German that I knew meant drop your rifle and I did."

"Then he yelled over to his captain, '"Sir, I caught me that Jerry pilot! Shall I send him to Valhalla?"'

"I'm no fucking German, you twit. I'm a Yank," I yelled back at him.

"I bet that convinced him you were an allied airman."

"Not really. He raised the rifle's muzzle swiftly to an inch from my nose. My nose seems to attract gun barrels…he had this 'I don't believe you look' in his eyes."

"It appears that you were in a sticky mess, Tommy."

"If his captain hadn't come up to look me over and dispatch the sergeant to check out the enemy's abandoned position, I think I would have lost the argument."

"You mean he would have shot you?"

"I believe so because the captain, Captain McDonald, informed me that they and the Germans had been at it for two days and nights before I showed up. They took a great many casualties. They weren't sure who I belonged to after those bullets went whistling over their heads and they didn't want to take any chances. As he assisted me out of the crater and walked me towards the abandoned position of the Germans, I told him of the four men I killed. I surmised that I had pissed someone off.

"The sergeant pointed out the last man I killed…the one who had been yelling and pointing at me. Seems I picked off a German general officer."

"Well done Thompson," the Captain remarked as he cut the epaulets off the general's uniform. He handed one to me and kept one to file with his after action report.

"The Brits dropped me off at an aid station where they put stitches in my arm and leg. The Boodles gin the corpsman gave me was a good anesthetic. After a couple healthy swigs from that bottle those pin pricks didn't faze me at all. I hadn't realized that I was cut on the arm until the medic complained that I was bleeding on his paper work. An empty seat was available on an ambulance heading east, and I was back in my unit at Deux Jumeaux, France, shortly thereafter.

"So that's my war story. Being involved in that ground action made the war a hell of a lot more personal. It made me aware of my mortality. I never thought about dying before, but that shelling scared the living bejesus out of me."

Tommy hesitated and chose not to mention he felt he was pulled out of that darkness by some voice that kept saying …"*It's not your time, hang on to me and I'll take you back to where you belong*," then my body was revitalized. The feeling was momentary but powerful.

The elderly driver didn't say any thing for a minute or two.

Finally he asked, "What's your last name, son?"

"Thompson, sir."

"Any relation to T.C. Thompson over at Thompson Industries?"

"My father," snapped Tommy. "If you know him, don't tell him that story. He won't believe you."

"Tommy, my last name is Peters and I want you to know that your story has sent a chill up my spine. I'm amazed that you went through that action and that the army is going to send you back."

"Mr. Peters, there are a great number of American soldiers who sacrificed a hell of a lot more than the few drops of blood that I did. And those that weren't killed and can still do those chores required of a soldier will be back in action when I am. I'm no better or worse then they are. We're not heroes, we're American fighting men doing the best we can." There were ten miles of silence as Tommy and Horatio both pondered his remarks.

The old driver shook Tommy's hand just before he dropped him off at the grocery store. He barely caught a glimpse of Peggy as she ran from the store screaming with delight. She was lost in his embrace as they fell laughing into a snow bank. "Lucky fellow," thought Peters as he pulled away. At the outskirts of town, he stopped, turned on the overhead dome light and wrote his thoughts, in outline form, on his spiral note book. He wanted to ensure that the story he heard from the young lad would stay fresh in his mind as he wrote his column for the city's weekly newspaper. He hoped that the kid hadn't let his mouth overload his ass because the story would make good reading. In his mind, he saw the lead-in announcing "We are not heroes." He didn't want to get the kid in trouble, but even if he did, his daddy would bail him out. Turning the light off as the car moved forward, Horatio settled back for the long ride home thinking, that's one lucky kid, and I'm one lucky old fart. The trouble started a couple days later when Peggy and Tommy's father read the newspaper.

Chapter 9

"Get that reporter on the phone and find out where he dropped off my son," he yell at his secretary.

"What reporter, Mr. Thompson?"

"The one that wrote this story," he shouted, throwing the newspaper at her. "What the hell kind of a reporter is he anyway? Didn't give the name of the town where he left him off. Didn't he think I would want to know that? If he gives you any of that military secret crap…tell him…no, just ask him, please." He went back into his office, closed the door, fell to his knees and whispered, "Thank you Lord."

* * *

Tommy was trying to convince Peggy's mother and father that he was the perfect man for their daughter. Her father kept arguing. "She's too young. She's got a scholarship to the University of Wisconsin. And Tommy, you're too fearless…I don't want her to be a teenage widow."

"But sir, I'm a damn good pilot."

"Hell Tommy, you've already been shot down twice."

"Yes but by ground fire…not by an enemy aircraft."

Good old dad was overruled three to one.

In the end, all agreed to the marriage with the stipulation that Peggy was to finish college.

"Tommy, let me see your arm. Roll up that sleeve," Peggy demanded as she held the city newspaper that had just been dropped off at the store.

Reluctantly he revealed the jagged scar on his bicep. Peggy brushed her lips gently over the scar and said "Roll up that pant leg!"

"Let me see that paper," Tommy pleaded.

"Better yet, let's all read that article," mother Mary Hanover interjected.

"Peggy if you're going to kiss his wounds to make them better, I hope for your sake he didn't take a round in his butt," offered her grinning dad.

"This is for your fatherly concern, John!" Mary said as she swatted his backside with the newspaper.

After they all read the article, everyone started shaking their heads, a faint gasp was heard from the women, and a barely audible "oh, hell" from Tommy. He noticed the article's byline and recognized Horatio Peters name. "I knew that telling my war story to that grungy old man was a rather large mistake," admitted Tommy.

Christmas Help

Her dad just looked at Tommy thinking his fearless future son-in-law has a rough road ahead of him and that his daughter's future of nights of loneliness and endless tears.

"My combat experience in the Great War left me with a philosophy that I want to share with you. Son, without luck, one's skill does not mean shit." This was a statement that Bartholomew wholeheartedly agreed with.

Not another word was spoken until Tommy broke the silence with, "May I have a cup of coffee?"

"Yes you can," Mary said as she brought the coffee pot, some hot cinnamon rolls and a couple sticks of butter and set them on the table just as the bells over the store door jingled. "John would you tend to that customer?" Mary asked as she poured the coffee. John was quick to go up to the front of the store and was a little taken aback as he observed a well-dressed man who appeared to be an older image of his future son-in-law. The two men stood there staring at each other until Mary came in, took one look and said "Mr. Thompson, we're just about to sit down with Tommy for a cup of coffee. Will you please join us?"

"I'm not sure if Tommy would be comfortable with me at the table."

"Since it's my table, he damn well better get over it," and with a quick move, she grabbed Mr. Thompson's arm and escorted him into the kitchen. "Tommy," she announced, "pull up a chair for your father."

"Dad?"

"Son!"

"Cream and sugar?" asked Peggy.

"Yes, please," he replied faintly.

For the first time in his life Tommy saw tears in his father's eyes. "Try the cinnamon rolls. They're exceptional, Dad." A tear swelled in his eye but did not drop.

And there, in that warm kitchen surrounded by Peggy's loving family, eight years of resentment and bitterness between father and son started to fall like the first leaves from an autumn tree…some fell freely and others stubbornly held fast. The relief from the anxiety of loving his father who had never showed his true feelings was almost pure pleasure. The three Hanovers seemed taken aback not knowing the history between these two future family members, but they let the silent drama play out without interruption for several minutes. Then Mary, her chin resting on her folded hands, asked, "Has your son told you of his intention to marry our daughter, Peggy?"

"No, he didn't, but I'm sure it is the best decision he has ever made in his life. If his mother hadn't passed away when he was ten years old, she would be the first to offer best wishes to Peggy, and welcome her into our family, and I would be second."

Tommy was relieved and beamed at his father's acceptance of his plan to marry Peggy.

The rest of the morning was filled with wedding plans that mother and daughter were arranging. The groom-to-be tried to make some suggestions, but it became clear from the way that the ladies rolled their eyes at his suggestions that the only details required of him were the location of the honeymoon and to be on time at the church in his class "A" uniform.

"Tommy how many guests from your side of the family do you want to invite? We are not planning a large affair. May be a hundred and fifty or so"

"Dad do you have a number that Mary could use for planning?"

"Would thirty five be too much of a burden, Mary?" suggested the senior Thompson.

"That number would be perfect," answered Mary.

"Mr. Thompson, would you be so kind to host the wedding party's rehearsal dinner? Mary asked as she looked up from her planning book.

"It would be my honor to host this event. Would two nights before the wedding be a suitable time?"

"That too would be perfect," answered Mary.

During his father's replies Tommy held his breath. He was nervous that his father's event would be so lavish that Mary and John would be embarrassed.

The two fathers excused themselves and went to the front of the store where the groom's father asked, "Where's a suitable place to hold the rehearsal dinner John, and will you let me know when the date is set for the wedding?"

"I think the Moose Hall would be appropriate because

the cook is excellent, and they have a private dining room large enough to accommodate the wedding party and a few selected guests. I'll notify you when the date is set in cement."

John suggested, "These women don't need us for their nut and bolt planning. Let's take a walk over to the hall so you can get an idea of the layout. We'll pass by the church, St. Teresa's, where the wedding will take place if the church will allow an exception to the posting of the "intent to marry." Seems they want three months' notice, and we're giving them only ten days."

"John, my mother had this irrational belief that every new church one went into, their wish would be granted. Do you think anyone will mind if I went in to test my mother's superstition?"

"Door's always open. I'll mosey on over to the hall and meet you there."

As the church door creaked open, Mr. Thompson was engulfed in a rainbow of colors emanating from the stained-glass window behind the altar in this cruciform shaped religious building. The scene depicted red roses petals descending onto the extended hands of mankind white, red, brown, yellow and black. The voice of Father Hurley, who was standing in the shadows next to a statue of Mary holding the Christ child, asked, "Do you know the symbolism of that window?

"No father, I don't."

"It's depicting a shower of rose petals falling on a

peaceful mankind. Don't know if a petal will fall in my life time but since our church is based on hope and forgiveness, maybe this will occur in your children's or grandchildren's children's times. Now, may I help you?"

"Yes, Father, you can. My son is going to marry Peggy Hanover in the next week. Her parents and I would like the wedding to take place in this church, but I am afraid if some obstacles can't be overcome, they will run to the nearest Justice of Peace and exchange their vows there. I know miracles can occur because my son and I have just spoken to each other for the first time in nine years and put aside a stupid riff that I caused."

Mr. Thompson's head was bowed and eyes were moist as Father Hurley replied, "Tell Peggy's parents that the wedding will be here on whatever date they select."

"Father, would it be too much of an imposition if you would tell them? I don't want them to think I injected my big fat butt into the church's business."

"I can do that."

"Thanks, Father." As he turned to leave, he took several hundred dollar bills from the money clip in his pocket, pressed them into the priest's hand and said, "Put a flower or two on the altar. I understand that St. Teresa is one of the patron saints for aviators. With your permission, may I light a candle for our boys who are flying and fighting for our freedom around the globe?"

"Yes, you may. Kneel here with me and we'll both ask for her intercession."

After the impromptu come to Jesus meeting, Mr. Thompson walked down the street to the Moose Hall where John Hanover introduced him to Bill Maddocks, the manager. The room for the rehearsal dinner party appeared to be adequate and the kitchen was spotless. The cook, Mike Conrad, was a very large man whose girth indicated he enjoyed eating the food that he prepared.

With pride, Conrad announced, "I can put on a nice spread of roast beef or baked chicken, mashed potatoes, gravy and two vegetables that won't put a big dent in your wallet."

Thompson, Sr., turned to John and asked, "Could your grocery store provide some prime rib and shrimp in time for the dinner?"

"I can do that," John replied.

"Mike is there a problem with John providing the meat and shrimp?

"Not for me. But Bill might object because there won't be much profit on this suggested arrangement."

"John, talk to Mike about the delivery schedule. I'll touch base with Bill."

"Will this arrangement work, Bill?"

"To tell you the truth I'm not going to make much of a profit with your suggested deal so I'm reluctant to agree."

"I like a man that doesn't mince word so I won't either. I'll give you twenty five dollars a plate and a hundred dollars for renting the room."

"Mr. Thompson, we have a deal," Bill said quickly as he realized the profit from an outrageous price per plate offered by Thompson, Sr.

"Bill, promise me that the tab will be confidential between you and me. Here's a couple extra hundred dollars to ensure there will be enough wait staff and linen available. Also I want wine and champagne glasses as part of the table arrangement. I'll provide the wine and champagne for the event. Here's my business card. Wait a minute give that back to me."

"Have you changed your mind?" asked Bill.

"Nope, I want you to have my home telephone number…I'll write it on the back. Call me if there's any problem, and please do not spread our agreement around town." He offered the card back to Bill.

The senior Thompson handed John a couple of bills on the way out the door and said, "This should cover the meat and shrimp, but if it doesn't, I'll settle up with you later."

John slid the bills back and forth between his fingers and said," If this doesn't take care of it, then I'm not much of a grocer."

The walk back was an opportunity for the two men to evaluate each other and neither found the other lacking in the qualities they considered important. Neither was a braggart, an egotist, or unduly impressed with himself. However both were surprised to discover they were former Marines who had served in World War 1.

"I was at Hill 142 and Belleau Wood," John remarked.

"Me too and I also made muster at Bouresches and Vaux," replied the senior Thompson.

"I missed that carnage because at Belleau Wood some stray shrapnel wiped me off my feet. Nothing very serious, I just couldn't walk for a few months. I consider my self very lucky as a hell of a lot of Marines didn't make it home," John observed.

"I noticed your limp John. Does it give you problems?"

"It did for the first couple years but now it only bothers me when the seasons change or when the temperature fall below zero…which is unfortunate because it occurs too damn often."

The bell rang as they stepped through the grocery store door. The senior Thompson summed their efforts during the war up with, "We paid our dues John. Semper Fi."

"You two wanderers get in here," ordered Mary. "The good Father dropped by and he's in the kitchen with Tommy and Peggy. John, bring that bottle of brandy you've tried to hide behind the jars of pickles."

"How does she do that?" John asked Thompson. "I was sure that I had found the perfect hiding place for my cough medicine."

"Obviously not," concluded a smiling Thompson.

"Yes, precious," a term that really pissed her off, John replied. During their twenty years of marriage he found that to head off any major confrontation all he had to do was acquiesce and say those two words. Even though the hairs on her neck would rise she allowed him these minor victories.

Father Hurley was just about to finish a rambling thought in his monologue when he spotted the bottle in John's hand and said, "Yes, don't mind if I do. And you must be the groom's father. Is that correct?" The good Father winked as he and the senior Thompson shook hands. John poured a round of brandy for all except Peggy, who declined on the grounds that even the fumes were enough to send her into Never, Never Land.

"I was just saying," continued Father Hurley, "that given the pressing circumstances of young Thompson's availability, I will dispense with the necessity of posting the intention to marry rule. You may marry on the date you have chosen. Now John, perhaps another splash of that fermented grape before I leave."

Three hours, another hidden bottle and supper later, Father Hurley, escorted by the two other fathers all singing "Danny Boy," found his way to the church parsonage where a toast to the coming nuptials was given several times!

The two fathers staggered back to the store singing, "It's a long way to Tipperary…" and as Thompson, Sr. struggled to un-lock the door to his 1941 Cadillac, Mary came up and snatched the keys from his hand. With her hands on her hips and her neck cranked back, she sternly announced, "I'm not going to let you run that car into some pine tree. Get in the house. The extra bed in the room Tommy is sleeping in is available and the covers are turned down. I'll wake you early if that's what you really want, but right now get in the house!"

He started to object but was cut short with another "get in the house" from an exasperated Mary. Opening the door to the house he sang," Mother, pin a rose on me..." and was rewarded with a snow ball on the back of his head. Silently he went to the bedroom, hardly aware of the snow melting down his neck. He flopped on the bed and was asleep before he had his neck tie off.

Chapter 10

The next morning an unexpected gift was delivered by a giant of a man. As he approached Mary and Peggy, Mary whispered to Peggy, "He stinks like burned pine wood…exactly like Tommy did the first time your father and I met him."

Joe Marsh handed a large bundle of silk parachute to Peggy's mother saying, "Maybe you could use it for your daughter's wedding dress or something."

Mary protested saying, "Peggy's going to wear my wedding dress, but I'm sure we can make one of the bridesmaid's dresses out of this, if you have no objection."

Joe blushed as he said, "You do what you want, pretty ladies. I just wanted to wish Peggy and Tommy a hundred years of happiness." Peggy reached up, stood on her tip toes, brought his head down and planted a big kiss on his forehead. Blushing a brighter red, he left in a big rush.

* * *

Tommy and his dad were returning from a walk they hoped would clear their heads and clear up some of the barriers that had surfaced between them in the years past. Halfway through the walk, near the highway rest pavilion that the WPA had erected, the senior Thompson grabbed Tommy's arm and demanded, "Tommy what did I do to alienate you?"

"Turn loose of my jacket and I'll tell you all you want to know and then some. For one thing it was that damn deer hunt…and how you never, not once, stopped telling that story…always laughing and mocking me."

Brushing the snow off the cement bench, "I didn't realize I was hurting you," Tommy's father replied, his voice filled with remorse. He sat with his fingers interlocked, his knuckles turning white trying to hold in his anger.

"You didn't hurt me physically. Your words were like sharp razors slicing away my love for you until the love was gone. With mom dead and you a stranger…a drunken stranger, I felt like an outcast," Tommy answered as he sat down next to his father.

"Me, a drunken stranger! I fed you, put clothes on your back, a roof over your head and worked my ass off to make the business a success. A business that will one day be yours. That's what a father does…not a stranger?"

His protesting remarks were louder than he intended and were not lost on his son."

"Hell dad, the army did most of those things for me and they didn't make me sick with the smell of a stinking, sour whiskey breath at breakfast."

"I have to admit I did and still do need a lot of sauce to make it through the night but there are reasons..."

Tommy interrupted, "You never shared those reasons with me. And then after mom's death, every Monday morning you would drop me off at Aunt Molly's house..."

His father's voice almost shouted, "What in the hell was wrong with that? I had to go to work and she was nice enough to try to help care for her sister's son. Did she beat you or mistreat you?"

"She never laid a hand on me, not even to hug me. Didn't you ever look at her and see she was almost mom's twin? Her blond hair. Her blue eyes. I looked at her and saw my mother. I looked at her and couldn't understand why God took mom and not her. Aunt Molly didn't have any kids and I guess she really didn't like kids. I hated Mondays."

"I can't justify my actions as a lousy, drunken father, but you have to admit you weren't exactly a boy scout growing up. Hell, you were into one mess after another. Like playing down at the creek and coming back to your Aunt Molly's with your wrist bleeding and blood all over your shirt and knickers. Your poor aunt almost fainted as the doctor put 20 stitches in that wound."

"I was just swinging on a tree limb over a small gully when the branch broke," Tommy said with his arms crossed tight around his chest.

"You always had an excuse when your plan didn't work out. Like, falling off your aunt's barn roof and breaking your arm."

"I didn't fall, the airplane I built out of those orange crates didn't fly."

"Is that what that pile of wood was…an airplane?"

"Yes sir, it was. Not as good and functional as the canoe I built later on, but I did build them all by myself."

"And how many people were in on your rescue when that damn black coffin sunk?"

"Just the two guys whose fishing I interrupted. I almost drank the whole lake dry because we were laughing so hard. I was tangled in their fishing lines and they had a large walleye hooked and didn't want to lose it. One would start to pull me into the boat and when their line went slack he would drop me back in so as not to lose that fish. It took three dunkings before they were able to net that fish and me."

"I thought the whipping I gave you cured all that boyhood foolishness. But then there were the cars. I don't know how in the hell you got the money to buy those old clunkers but Aunt Molly's barn is full of them. There's a 1934 Packard Touring machine, a 1936 four door Ford Convertible and at least a half dozen more in various stages of repair. Some how you got them running just long enough I suppose to kick up the dirt on those back roads. And the aunt that you say never hugged you, she's the one who protected you by never telling me what you were up to."

"With Aunt Molly it was a financial arrangement. She would lend me the money and I would pay her back with interest. I was running errands for all the little old ladies that couldn't get around due to their age. They would tip me. I never asked for a penny but they would always press a dime or quarter in my hand. After a while some of the stores had me making deliveries and would pay me a quarter or so a trip. I did this after school before you picked me up."

"I never caught on to your business venture just as I never figured out why you left with out saying good by, thanks for that 1940 Buick convertible you left behind or kiss my ass."

"Dad, when the Japanese bombed Pearl Harbor I was going to join the army and figured you wouldn't agree to that move. I thumbed my way to Madison and signed up. Then I thought it best to drop the charade of son and father and get on with the real war. My actions weren't the brightest moves I've made, sort of on the same level as my attempt at airplane building , but I was pig headed and refused to think about it. I apologize for any hurt I caused you dad. I hope Aunt Molly will forgive me for not saying goodbye."

"She passed away two months after you left."

Tommy put his face in his hands and after a very quiet minute mumbled, 'The consequences of my actions are infinite. And the one I am most truly sorry for is not being home to say goodbye to Aunt Molly. What happened to her Dad?"

"She had a weak heart from her bout with rheumatic fever as a child and it failed one night as she slept. She adored you but didn't have the strength to hold you like she wanted."

"Those gentle pats on my head…I guess were her love taps. I was just too stupid to recognize them for what they were," a crushed young warrior confessed.

"She left you everything she owned Tommy, which included that barn full of old clunkers, the house, two hundred acres of farmland and a shoe box full of stock certificates in a telephone company and the car company that makes Chevys. I have allowed a married couple to live in the house and farm the property on a fifty-fifty basis…with your approval, I hope."

"Your arrangement is fine with me, Dad. I truly wish I had known that she was that fragile. She never let on that she wasn't well. As a kid I wasn't really as observant as I should have been."

"It appears that trait runs in the family, son."

"Maybe it was the booze Dad, maybe it was your work that kept us apart, but as a kid I thought it was me."

"Son, we've both been to war and seen and done things that will stay with us forever…we're cut from the same cloth and the blood that flows through our bodies binds us together whether we like it or not. We can't change the past, God knows I would give my soul for a chance to have been a good father to you as you grew up. But that's not going to happen. That's yesterday. Perhaps if you're willing, we can start today, start right now to work towards a closer and happier relationship. Can we do that Tommy?"

"Dad I'm willing because I want to love you and be a member of the family again. But mostly I want Peggy to know that she can depend on us come hell or high water."

They continued their walk, not hand in hand or arm in arm but with an occasional glance at each other trying to gauge what effect their words had on the other.

Tommy waved down his friend, Joe, driving his dilapidated truck on his way out of town. Joe stopped and got out. "Come here little fella," he said, giving Tommy a bear hug that took Tommy's breath away.

"Dad, this is Joe Marsh, the man who pulled me out of the airplane, hauled my ass out of the creek then put me up in his cabin and fed me for three days."

Joe responded, "Your son was one hell of a woodsman and my offer of a job after the war still stands."

An amazed senior Thompson looked at this bear of a man who saved his son, then glanced at his truck and asked, "Are you coming to the wedding?"

"Haven't been asked," replied Joe.

"Be my best man, and you'll have one of the best seats in the church," Tommy begged.

"Come blizzard or flood, I'll be there," said Joe pulling away in a thick cloud of black exhaust smoke.

The days flew by as preparations were completed by the family, and the wedding rehearsal was a light-hearted affair. Father Hurley acted as the master of ceremonies with a flair that none of the church members remembered from past church activities. His actions may have been influenced by the drinking session he had that afternoon with the other two fathers.

"We have gone through the ceremony several times and I want to congratulate you all on performing your parts with the skill and dexterity of the Norte Dame football team's backfield. Joseph you are quite light on your feet and I want you sober on the big day because if you trip and fall you'll wipe out the entire bridal party."

"Not a sip will pass my lips that morning Father, and that's a promise good from sunup to lunch time."

"Now Peggy and Tommy...after the ceremony and before you leave the altar, I want you two to kiss. Show me how you intend to do that."

As they embraced Father Hurley said, "No, No, No! Step back and try again. Tommy this is your wife you will be kissing, not your mother in law."

Tommy held her closely and was sure he was doing it correctly until Peggy started to laugh. "Okay you two, that was unacceptable. Peggy this is serious business, no more giggling. And Tommy keep your tongue in your mouth. One more time."

They kissed three more time before Father Hurley announced, "There are so very few things in this world that are perfect, but as Christ as our witness, that kiss was perfect. Alright, it is time for the dinner party. I don't want to be the object of your mother's wrath for holding up the festivities, so scoot and I'll follow in just a minute."

The short walk in the cold crisp air took only five minutes and all welcomed the warm atmosphere in the club.

"Peggy, is this really the Moose Hall? Look at the linen and the flowers on the table. They are beautiful… and the long stem glassware. How really nice, almost elegant," Mary marveled.

"Mom, where did they get the candleholders? They are so impressive."

Tommy was quick to answer, "If I was to guess, they're my grandmother's." He glanced at his dad who turned to Bill and said, "Well done."

The party room reflected the attention to detail that Bill insisted his employees give to this occasion. He wanted the arrangements to please his friends the Hanovers, the bride and groom, and in particular the man with the money. The table for twenty-one was set in perfect order. And well it should be, as he had a picture from Emily Post's book to guide his staff as they duplicated it with precision. The candleholders and flowers had been delivered that afternoon by one of Mr. Thompson's employees. The wine was being poured as the guests arrived and were being seated.

Tony Skur

Father Hurley's prayer was short and to the point, "Heavenly Father, we thank you for the bounty we are about to share and the Blessings you have given to all of us. Unite these two families as they come to celebrate the marriage of their children. We ask this through Christ, our Lord, amen."

Before the priest could sit, John raised his glass of wine and said, "Before I toast to bride and groom, I would like to remind them about love:

Love is a nod from across the room.
Love is a knowing wink.
Love is a laugh from the heart's full bloom.
Love is a pause to think
Selflessly, wholly, of what it shares.
Threaded by man and wife,
Quietly weaving 'til unawares
Love is the whole of life."

At this point John's mind went blank and the groom's father stood and continued:

"Love is an arm to support an arm.
Love wipes a way a tear.
Love speaks of love with a special charm.
Love is a list'ning ear.
Love is the squeeze of a gentle hand,
Saying what words can't say.
Knowing such love makes one understand
God in a wiser way."

The two fathers look at each other smiling and in unison said, "To the bride and groom."

Mary looked at them with admiration and said, "I can't believe you two share a fondness for Margaret Rorke's poem. I believe I will raise my estimation of you two that suffered when you both came home last night drunk as any bum I've ever seen in my life."

"John, I believe we are on the road to Mary's good graces. I for one will try to be 'good as any angel from above' that I'm acquainted with. A toast to our recently raised status," Mr. Thompson offered as he raised his glass.

"Cheers, and welcome to our family," John replied with great enthusiasm.

"Welcome to the Thompson family," responded both Thompsons, Sr. and Jr.

The group acknowledged the toasts and were rewarded with another glass of wine as a shrimp cocktail was served. The senior Thompson and John were gracious hosts throughout the meal as they engaged the guests in witty and cheerful conversation. Mary couldn't believe the size of the prime rib cut and with a look of inquisitiveness on her face, nudged John who shrugged his shoulders and quietly said, "I'm a better grocer than I thought I was."

Joe Marsh was on his best behavior, his table manners were impeccable, and his ability to manage the fork with his three fingers was amazing. His dinner conversation was witty and not one word of his logger's language past his lips. He beamed when Mary cut her slice of prime rib almost in half and with a stealthy movement placed the larger portion on his plate. When Peggy placed half of her slice on his plate, Joe's smile lit up the room.

His six foot eight inch frame unfolded as he rose and lifted his glass to honor the bridal party, "There is in this world a conflict that is separating families, but we are here to celebrate the joining of two families and the bringing together of their beautiful children. May the angels that look after fighter pilots keep Tommy safe, and may the angels that protect students, keep her absorbed in her studies while he is away."

A chorus of "cheers to Tommy and Peggy" ended his toast.

Bartholomew wanted to add, *Be not afraid children, I will do my job*, but the only evidence of his toast was the flickering of the candles' flames.

Just when all were thinking they were satisfied with their dinner and couldn't hold another bite, a hot piece of apple pie with ice cream was placed before them and coffee was served.

Bill came into the room and asked in a quiet tone, "Mr. Thompson, I have a small band in the main room. I'd like them to start if they won't disturb your party."

"The only way they would disturb us is if we are not invited to dance."

"Your party is more than welcome."

"Did I send enough champagne so that everyone in the hall could have a glass?"

"Yes, you did."

"Then at the first band break, please pour, and we will have a another toast to the bride and groom from every one in the hall."

Later in the evening "Last call," from the bartender was received with a groan from the crowd. As wives and sweethearts pulled at arms of their escorts encouraging them to leave, the senior Thompson pulled Joe aside and led him to a sparkling 1941 Ford ton and a half stake body truck, that his mechanic brought to town and placed in the parking lot. He looked up at Joe and said, "This truck hasn't been getting much use at my factory. My mechanic has looked it over and pronounced it fit and ready for duty."

"What kind of duty?" a suspicious Joe asked as he kicked the front left tire.

"The kind of duty where you pluck fighter pilots out of the woods. Here's the keys and the title. You already have my appreciation for taking care of my son after he crashed in the woods. Now take the damn truck, and I'll see you at the wedding."

Bewildered, Joe took the keys and title. No one had ever given him a thing. That is, if you don't count those ladies who, on occasion, favored him with some free love. He grasped his benefactor's hand, gave it one big shake, mumbled "thanks" and produced a bottle of snowshoe grog from his jacket pocket. "Maybe one for the road," he offered.

"All right, Joe, just one." That one turned out to be several.

They sat quiet as mice in the cab of the truck. Mr. Thompson looked at Joe's mangled hand and joked, "Are the missing fingers a result of a misguided axe?"

"No sir! Just the result of a disagreement between me and a German infantry man during the last big war," Joe replied as he handed the bottle to Thompson.

"You were too damn young be in that war to end all wars," Thompson remarked with unveiled sarcasm. He took a long swig from the half empty bottle.

Joe's smiling face turned grim as he recalled a time twenty five years ago. "I had just turned fifteen when my old man kicked me out of the house because I ate too much. I was a tall lad, almost six foot six, and had hair around my private parts… so the physical was easy to pass when I went to enlist in the army two days later. I was probably the only recruit in the army that didn't complain about the chow. Those cooks looked at my size and gave me an extra scoop of whatever was in the pot," answered Joe a defensive edge on his voice.

"So when did you lose the fingers?" the senior Thompson persisted.

"On the sixteenth of July, 1918 during the battle at Marne. The German artillery had stopped and the sun's rays barely broke through the smoke and dust." Joe recalled.

Christmas Help

"Are you going to tell me how you lost your fingers or are you going to tell me the visibility was bad?" an impatient senior Thompson asked.

"The dust was settling when the Germans overran our trench. There was a lot of hand to hand fighting, yelling, and screaming from both sides. This young German trooper came after me, rifle in hand with the bayonet attached. He wasn't much older than me and a damn site smaller…except for his rifle that made him seem ten feet tall. Why he didn't shoot I can't even guess. I sidestepped his trust and made a grab for his rifle but caught his bayonet with my right hand. There was a sharp pain and when I looked, I was missing a couple of fingers. Then I got pissed and grabbed him by the throat, lifting that little bastard off the ground holding him there until his neck broke. And then I went a little nuts and started down that trench smearing my blood on the enemies' faces. I broke the necks of every fucking German I could get my eight fingers on. Pass the bottle," an almost sober Joe Marsh muttered.

Silence surrounded them for a couple minutes as they finished the snowshoe grog. Mr. Thompson grabbed Joe's deformed hand and remarked, "Buddy, I'm proud that you were the man that saved my son and are going to be his best man. I know the pain from that war isn't always physical. I was a machine gunner with the 6th Marine machine gun battalion. In eight battles I never got a scratch, but I put down more men then there are in this town. I hate remembering that madness. My stomach tightens and the bile floats up my throat. The worst part is those battles creeping into my mind when I try to sleep. Most nights it takes a half a bottle of whiskey to get some shut eye. I've never shared this nightmare with Tommy. Maybe I should."

He waved as Joe drove with great care, but not quite straight down the road. Then he stumbled along the road, not quite straight towards the grocery store. He was thankful that Mary reserved the bed in Tommy's room for him. There were no nightmares this night of long ago battles. He slept the sleep of an absolved repentant sinner.

Chapter 11

On the appointed day, at the appointed hour, the church door opened as the organist began Handel's Wedding March. Tommy turned to watch his bride come forward out of a backdrop of dazzling sunlight. She brought with her a radiant glow that forced a lump to his throat. The best man, Joe Marsh, squinted through a black eye suffered back at the logging camp where one of his men called him a liar after Joe bragged that someone had given him the truck. He had to wipe his good eye with his red bandana to hold the tears back. Peggy's father placed his daughter's hand on Tommy's arm and whispered, "She may soon be your wife, but she will always be our daughter. Take care of her always."

Father Hurley made sure the ceremony was conducted with perfection, reflecting what was rehearsed. The perfect kiss after the vows were exchanged ended the ceremony.

The reception that evening at the hall in the church's basement was Mary's event of pride and joy. From the flowers brought downstairs after the ceremony, the polka band's lively music, the bountiful buffet, to the open bar, it was all her doing. The evening could not have been more enjoyable. The bride and groom greeted everyone at the door with a handshake or hug and were rewarded with the customary white envelope, which they placed in a decorated box. Inside the envelopes were money gifts to help the newlyweds get started in their life together. The guests immediately went to the bar, where the ladies ordered a "seven and seven," and the men called for a "shot of whiskey with a beer back." It soon became apparent that there were more guests than the number invited, but each trespasser handed a white envelope to the bride or groom. Wondering what to do about the lack of food for these uninvited guests, Mary looked at John who shrugged his shoulders as he lifted his tumbler to his lips. The senior Thompson became aware of the problem and with discretion asked, "John, may I help?"

"Mary and I would be most thankful if you would."

Mr. Thompson slipped over to the Moose Hall, consulted with Bill, and with Mike's help, they put together tray after tray of food which were quickly spirited into the church's kitchen and added to buffet line.

"Mr. Thompson, the bar is running a little dry. With your approval I can also fix that," whispered Bill.

"Do it and hand me the tab. You will not mention the cost to anyone."

"No one can pry that information from me, sir." With

that promise Bill provided the bar with ample reserves to quench the thirst of the party's revelers, invited or not. They were a dancing crowd, especially the best man. Joe whirled every woman around the floor at least once and the single ladies a couple times more. For a large man, he was a capable dancer who was able to circle and lift his partners off the floor with an ear splitting "e i e i o." Remarkably, there were no fights. If an angry voice was raised, Joe and his three uninvited woodsmen helpers would walk up to the offending parties and glare at them. Peace prevailed.

Tommy and Peggy left the reception about midnight and made a beeline for a cabin in the woods that John and Mary owned. The short dirt road up to the cabin had been snow plowed. Tommy carried his bride the last ten feet through the foot deep snow. Stomping his feet to shed the snow, he looked over the one room building. Someone had started a blazing fire in the fireplace. A bottle of champagne with two tulip glasses were on the night stand. The down comforter was turned down, revealing an inviting bed. The suitcase they brought with them had been tampered with and contained only one pajama top and a nighty that a mischievous mother had shortened. Attached to the hem was a border of parachute material stenciled with Property U.S. Army Air Corps. The border hem was lined with fox tails. The note pinned to the garment stated, "to keep your neck warm."

And indeed it did.

Chapter 12

Gray, oily smoke bellowed from the right engine of the C-47 as the co-pilot advanced the throttle out of the cut off position. The blustery north wind at Truax Field dispersed the vapor and fumes into the snow flurries, causing them to disappear before they encompassed the couple embracing in front of the passenger terminal.

The pilot in command gripped the left throttle, holding it in the stop position. He shouted over the irritating exhaust noise, "Let's give those two love birds a little more time to hold their bodies close together. The Flight Officer is going back to France and it'll be a while until he's back with her…if he's lucky enough to make it back at all."

"I can't believe thirty days could evaporate with such quickness," Tommy said as he wiped a tear from Peggy's eye. He whispered as their cheeks touched each other, "Don't worry about me, I'm good at what I do, but I'll take as many prayers as you want to give me. I love you, Peggy."

All Peggy could get past the restriction in her throat was, "Oh Tommy, I love you so much," and then he was gone, his plane disappearing in the swirling snow.

His connections with aircraft going east were unfortunate in that they were just as good as his rides home had been. In three days, he was back at his unit, and after one day of briefings on the current situation, his aircraft's wheels were coming to the up position. He was in a combat mode and ready for what ever lay ahead.

His selection to lead flights searching for targets of opportunity gave Tommy license to attack anything that moved. During the first week in November he managed to find, through some daring flying fifty feet above the railroad tracks, three locomotives. They were passing through the Black Forest highlands in southwestern Germany. The hundred foot high trees had kept them hidden until Tommy's wingman, Amos Jackson, flying top cover, called out on a static filled radio, "Lead there's smoke coming through the trees a mile in front of you!"

"Two, your timing is perfect. I have the target in sight and have rockets on the target." Pulling up into a cloud of flames, smoke and small pieces of locomotive, Tommy felt his asshole tighten as the metal pieces rattled the horizontal stabilizer. At that moment, he felt he could snap the heads off of ten penny nails with his anus.

"Lead, I see another one a mile or so down the tracks."

"Okay Amos, he's yours. I have to check out my controls," Tommy replied as he gingerly put some "G" forces on his aircraft. The aircraft appeared to handle well as Tommy watched his wingman demolish his target. "Two, I see another one just up the road going into a tunnel. I'll put my bomb on it and close this side. Go to the other side of the mountain and wait for him to exit. I'm going to strafe the cars that are still upright."

"Lead, your machine guns' popping almost blocked your transmission. I'll wait for him to exit if that's what you want."

"Affirmative, affirmative, that's what I want!" Tommy yelled as he came off his pass.

Tommy arrived at the target just as his wingman's five hundred pound bomb hit the side of the tunnel. The locomotive plowed through the mud and snow as if the track was clear. Tommy rolled in with his rockets corkscrewing past the trains engine into the covered railroad cars. His wingman salvoes of all his rockets on the steam engine with spectacular results. At first the scene looked like Old Faithful at Yellow Stone Park. Then a second later the scene was reminiscence of Dante's Inferno. The flames blackened the squadron's identification stripes on the fuselage. Tears filled Amos' eyes were the result of the acrid smoke seeping into the cockpit. They were wiped away with his not so white scarf.

"Amos join on me...my bird's acting a little dicey."

"Lead, you have nice collection of German Railway car pieces hanging from your tail section. You better handle that beast as if you were milking a mouse."

His reputation as a "magnet ass" intact, he brought all those holes and scrap iron home to Deux Jumeaux, one of the allied air patches in France.

"You're a lucky rascal Mr. Thompson," his crew chief noted. "This piece of brass bell damn near cut your elevator cable in two. If you don't want it, I would like to keep it so that folks will know that this Juggernaut lives up to its name."

"It's yours," answered a blushing Tommy.

Bartholomew was slightly peeved thinking, *Krishna didn't have a damn thing to do with this flight…then he remembered that Juggernaut was the name given by the manufacturer to this crushing force of an air machine.* His ruffled feathers now laid smoothly in place.

Winter times' light snow flurries were barely visible as Tommy and his favorite wingman, Flight Officer Amos Jackson, walked briskly out to their awaiting aircrafts two weeks before Thanksgiving. The squadron operations officer kept these two tigers scheduled together because they found targets when his other sharp eyed pilots missed them. The squadron commander, on the other hand, kept his fingers crossed when he saw this pairing thinking it was only a matter of time before he would have to write a…sorry to inform you letter … to their survivors.

"Think we'll be able to top these snow clouds?" inquired Amos blowing away a snowflake that had landed on his map.

"The old weather wizard looked in his crystal ball and

guessed they topped out at 3,000 feet. If he's right, we'll climb up to 5,000 above the freezing rain level and cruise out towards Bastogne and see if we can stir the pot. If not, we'll come down to where we can fly visually. Just hang in there, and maybe we'll get lucky and find us a juicy target or two," quipped Tommy.

The luck that prevailed had them bouncing in the clouds at 8000 feet for 70 miles, then they came out of the clouds to a clear condition but with only a mile or two visibility.

"This smoke from what's left of the industrial complex and the haze doesn't make for good bird hunting," muttered a disappointed Amos who had hoped to tangle with some German aircraft.

"Check two o'clock low. Forget the birds. Let's use our rockets on the train."

"Lead's in."

"Two roger, and in to your right."

The pass was successful, but the orange flames from the burning train added more smoke to the lousy visibility. As he started his pull-up, Tommy spotted a B-24 Liberator bomber a mile away in his nine o'clock position flying at 150 feet. Two of his four radial engines were out and one of the good ones was trailing black smoke.

"Green two, do you have that bomber in sight? He's nine o'clock low."

"Roger lead, I also have a visual on two bandits closing in on his tail."

The Liberator's pilot, Captain Joe Powell, struggled to keep his aircraft in the air. The "Wolf Pack" of German ME-109's had decimated his nine-member crew, three killed, four wounded and all defensive guns rendered useless. The trailing smoke from his right outboard engine pointed to his aircraft like an arrow. Occasionally a bright flame could be seen lapping at the engine's nacelle. The wolverine game the enemy fighters performed in the sky was a dance of death.

The sun's rays sparkled off the ME-109's windscreen giving Tommy the advantage of seeing the enemy and not being seen. The results of his 135 degree deflection shot at the lead fighter from his lower altitude amazed both Tommy and the Luftwaffe pilot who didn't have time to verbalize the German equivalent of "oh shit" as his aircraft disintegrated. Tommy rolled his aircraft upside down trying to avoid the debris, and lo and behold, there was the German's wingman closing nose to nose with him. From his inverted position and zero degrees deflection, he fired a three second burst from his eight 50 caliber Browning machine guns. The burst of bullets shattered the propeller and cockpit of the ME 109. Tommy sailed over his opponent, cockpit to cockpit, and was surprised to see flames engulfing the slumped over body. He rolled ninety degrees and pulled a six-G climbing turn into the sun hoping his wingman was able to hang in there.

"Two, say position."

"4:30, 50 yards, bomber low at 200 yards. By the by,

lead, there are two more bandits pulling in for the kill on the bomber's tail," he radioed.

"Lead's got them in sight. They must have their heads up their ass. They don't see us. I'm in."

Gently lowering the nose and easing in twenty degrees of bank, his curve of pursuit was text book perfect. I've been living right, Tommy thought as he squeezed the trigger. Then again, maybe not so right. Nothing happened. "Oh, oh," he mumbled to himself. Recycling his switches he begged, "Come on…come on… fire…damn it… fire." Nothing. He looked up. He was going to overshoot, he pushed forward on the stick and slid under the ME 109 and headed for the tree tops to avoid giving his enemy an easy shot. He was about to tell "two" to take on the fighter when Amos interjected.

"Splash the lead, going after his number two. Tommy, can you turn easy left?"

"Yes, but I'm not crazy about being bait." He reluctantly complied as the sound of his wing man's bullets in his head set were chalking up Amos's second victory in less than fifteen seconds.

"Two, take the bombers' left side I'll take his right." As they drove into position, Tommy rechecked his guns. Damn, they were still jammed.

"Amos, how are your guns? Mine are kaput."

"Lead, mine are fucking perfect."

"Amos, have we run into a bunch of student pilots, or are we just that damn good?"

"Lead, we're really that damn good. And there is a flight of four bogeys ten o'clock high."

"Beautiful. Just fucking beautiful. Join on me." Tommy started a turn, but he recognized the red tail fighters as P-51's from the Tuskegee black airman's fighter squadron heading west.

"Disregard two, those four are friendlies. Take up your position on the left side of the bomber. We'll escort him home," ordered Tommy.

They stayed with the bomber over the turbulent North Sea. "Tommy, do you think this thing can stay airborne much longer. If they have to bail out or ride it down that water will be just as deadly as those German pilots' bullets. They probably wouldn't last a half hour in that churning cold sea."

"Not much we can do for them. Let's just hang in there with them to give them moral support."

In addition to the two engines shot out, there was a three-foot long, two feet wide hole in the fuselage forward of the vertical stabilizers. Tommy could look through the hole and see Amos on the other side of the bomber. Additionally, one of the horizontal stabilizers was missing its top half. "Well Amos, I hope your fellow Texans in Fort Worth said a prayer with every rivet they put into this Liberator. They could use a little divine intervention."

Sorry gentlemen I'm here only for Tommy, a frustrated Bartholomew rationalized.

The sea and air seemed to calm. *"That wasn't me Lord."*

"I know that Bartholomew. I just answered thousands of prayers from those lady riveters in Cowtown."

One hour later with the runway in sight, a sweat soaked Joe Powell waved farewell to the two fighter pilots, assured in his mind that they must be absolutely insane. Diverting the enemy fighters from their intended target caused him to doubt their sanity but not their valor. He whispered "Thanks" into a dead microphone, and at that moment, Tommy waved and thought, *Good luck.*

"Aircraft on final approach at Station 120, you are cleared to land."

"Jake, fire some green flares. This one's radio isn't working," commanded Tech Sergeant Cassidy, the tower supervisor

"Flares in the air, boss, and crash vehicles in position," replied Staff Sergeant Jake Polaski as he fired a green flare from the Very pistol mounted in the roof of the tower. "Doesn't look like they're gonna make it. They're below the trees. My God. Somehow they've barely cleared the trees at the end of the field…whoops…only one landing gear's down!"

Inside the damaged bomber it felt more like an arrival than a landing at Station 120 near Attlebridge, England. The heavily damaged aircraft stalled four feet higher than Powell planned, because the right engine stopped due to fuel starvation. The aircraft violently pivoted as the one landing gear dug into the grassy infield. The twin tail section twisted and separated from the fuselage, ending up with the tail gunner's position along side the cockpit. Powell couldn't remember if the tail gunner had brown or black hair. It didn't matter now as the top of his head was gone. He puked onto the instrument panel.

Releasing his seat belt and harness, Powell left his dead co-pilot at the controls as he staggered his way to the rear to help the wounded. Crash crews and medics were already taking the wounded out of the plane and doing their jobs with the ease that comes with too much experience. When all crew members were en route to the hospital, morgue, or debriefing, Powell sat down on the grass inhaling the sweet tobacco taste of a Lucky Strike cigarette.

"Damn, damn, damn," were the only words he could utter as he exhaled the cloud of cigarette smoke. A medic tapped him on the shoulder and suggested, "A little mission whiskey might be in order to calm your nerves, sir."

"Thanks, but I better go to debriefing first." Shoulders hunched, head down, he shuffled towards the debriefing room wishing for the company of his crew.

An hour later, back in France, Tommy and Amos were walking from the flight line to their debriefing tent. Amos came to a screeching stop, grabbed Tommy by his arm and asked, "Just what in the hell were you thinking when you turned towards those four bogeys with your guns jammed?"

"Well I wasn't going to be bait for your fishing expedition…maybe I could just ram one of their rudders…hell I don't know. Let's not debrief that part."

"And what do we fess up to on our 200 mile jaunt escorting that flying Swiss cheese back to his home base. I think the commander is not going to be happy with us gallivanting all over Europe."

"Damn it Amos, why do you want to take the fun out of this mission…we'll tell them I felt lucky and you being a disciplined wingman would follow your courageous leader to the gates of hell…but no further."

"Tommy, we were made to fly together," Amos said as he punched his leader on the arm.

Bartholomew just shook his head and prayed that his bag of tricks would last to the end of the war.

Chapter 13

Major Peck faced Flight Officers Thompson and Jackson, who were two bundles of nerves standing at a position of attention, in his office. "Gentlemen at ease, relax this won't hurt," he said with a twisted smile.

"Thompson, I thought you and Jackson had been drinking 100 proof alcohol when you claimed four victories. It seemed a little unreasonable until I reviewed your wing camera's film. Then I received this recommendation for a valor award from a Captain Joe Powell of the 466th. In light of your accomplishments, not only do I concur with the recommendation, I have been authorized by the Wing Commander to tender a reserve commission with the rank of first lieutenant to both of you. Do you accept?"

Silence.

"Well do you?" Major Peck was an impatient man on the ground and in the air.

Amos looked at Tommy and suggested, "More money and we don't have to salute all the snotty nose second balloons. They salute us."

"Major, we accept," Tommy said with as straight a face as he could muster. He could barely contain the rush of joy that overwhelmed him. The smile that crept across his face was not lost on his commander.

"Our admin people have papers for you to sign and some silver bars to adorn your tunics. Good luck, Lieutenants. Tonight you buy the bar over at the Auger Inn." The inn was the officers' pub that was christened with that name as a reminder of their comrades whose luck ran out.

"There goes the first month's raise "came a bittersweet comment from Jackson.

"Could be worse," quipped Tommy. "They could be toasting our bones."

At the inn, there was a boisterous chorus of songs being sung. Over one hundred bright-eyed and bushy-tailed fighter pilots raised their voices to serenade the new lieutenants with a song, some thought originated during the first big war.

We loop in the silvery morning,
We spin in the purply dawn.
With a trail of black smoke behind us
to show where our leader has gone.
Oh lift your glasses gently
This world is a world of lies.
Here's to the dead already
And here's to the next man who dies.

As the last word lingered in the air, they all pointed at each other and chugged their drinks.

Chapter 14

"Hey Tommy, the Stars and Stripes newspaper says the war is almost over," Amos noted glancing up from the paper.

"I hope the Germans got a copy of that news report, particularly the panzer tank troops. Although we haven't seen hide nor hair of them the last few days, they are bound to be hiding somewhere. Maybe they went back to the Fatherland for the Christmas holidays. Hell, your guess is as good as the people running the war," kidded Tommy. The pair were waiting in the briefing room with twenty one other "Jug" drivers. All wondered if the weather would hold for the early morning mission. Tommy was scheduled to lead a flight of four in a twenty-four ship gaggle, with Amos as his element leader. The air was thick with cigarette smoke when the room was called to "attention" as the commander walked in.

"Seats, gentlemen," barked Major Peck. "I'll be leading this search-and-destroy mission. If it moves, it's a legitimate target. I'll circle the airfield at 5,000 feet until you are all in position. My call sign is Red one. White flight, with four aircraft, on my left; Blue flight with four aircraft, on my right; and Green Flight in trail with four aircraft, 200 feet low. Orange flight and Black flight left and right each with four aircraft, on Green Flight. I want Orange and Black flights to drop out first, fifteen minutes after we start northeast. Then in five-minute intervals, Green, Blue, and White will drop out. Start your patrols from a race track pattern ten miles long and two miles wide. Plan for a two-and-a-half hour sortie. Intelligence and weather men will now give their briefings. Good hunting."

"Although the allies are advancing on a broad front, there's strong German resistance in Belgium, and, in particular, around the town of Bastogne and the International Highway," Captain Fox the intelligence officer stated with conviction. "There'll be air activity, hopefully only ours, as C-47's and gliders try to resupply the ground troops. Some units of the 101st Airborne will be involved, and the Division commander would appreciate it if the fighters would stay clear of that area until called upon. Several sticks of pathfinder paratroopers, in groups of six or eight men, have been dropped beyond the perimeter of Bastogne and he doesn't want them killed by you fearless flyers thinking they are the enemy. As usual the anti-aircraft threat is the same, heavy small arms up to quad-fifty one caliber machine guns hidden in the most unlikely places. Also the panzer tank has that 88 millimeter gun that will spoil your day if you're unfortunate in spotting one after he detects you. My advice is keep that airplane moving around the sky and keep your head out of your ass. Good luck gentlemen"

The balding weather officer noted cheerfully "…that the clouds and visibility during this mission will hold so that all phases of your flight will be in visual flight conditions. The winds at five and ten thousand feet are out of the west at fifteen knots."

An audible sigh of relief from the gathering of anxious pilots.

"How some ever my forecast for mid December and beyond is not sunshine and tropical breezes. I anticipated low clouds, snow, low visibility and icing from two hundred to fifteen thousand feet during the last weeks in December." He was booed as he left the stage.

"Flight commanders, brief your crews," ordered Major Peck.

Chapter 15

The air was crisp and cold as Green Flight became airborne and put their wheels in the up position.

"Green Flight go button three," Tommy ordered.

"Green Flight check in."

"Two…Three…four."

The join-up of the twenty four aircraft took only two 360 degree turns, then Major Peck led the formation towards the assigned sector. Fifteen minutes later, Orange and Black flights eased out of the formation and, on cue, Green Flight descended from 5,000 feet.

"Green Flight button six," Tommy ordered the flight to change the radio frequency to one that they would have to themselves.

"Green Flight check in."

"Two…Three…Four

Tommy pushed on his rudder pedals, yawing his aircraft. This signaled his flight to spread into a tactical formation. When the wingmen could barely read the large squadron letters on the side of their lead's fuselage, they were to the correct position. With this fairly wide separation, the flight could maintain flight integrity and still search for ground activity.

After passing over the same farmhouse for he third time, Green three radioed, "I saw three or four men running from the out house to the farm house."

"Roger three, I'm in for a closer look" acknowledged Tommy as he rolled his aircraft inverted and went down for a closer look. That close look turned serious as ground fire racked Tommy's aircraft.

"Green Flight, take out the barn. They are stitching me," Tommy breathlessly exclaimed as he maneuvered his aircraft to get in trail with Green Four. The flight was like a one-eyed dog in a meat market as they dropped their 500-pound bombs on the barn. There was a bright flash as the barn roof came up to meet Green Three after he released his bombs on the gasoline truck parked next to a panzer tank. The gasoline truck's inferno spread over the tank and Green Four added to the destruction with his bombs.

Tommy started his second run as two nests of machine guns fired at him from the corners of the farmhouse. With his eight 50 caliber machine guns firing, he "walked" the bullets from one machine gun nest, through the house, to the second nest. He chandelled up to survey the area. A swarm of German infantry poured out of the house, trying to shoot in his direction. They did not see Green

Two, Three and Four coming in line abreast with twenty four machine guns fixed on their position. When Tommy made his third pass, not a round was fired at him and he counted thirty men lying silent on the frozen ground.

"Green Flight, join up and give me your status," Tommy barked over the radio.

"Two, rockets only, fuel sweet."

"Three, rockets only, fuel sweet."

"Four rockets only, fuel sweet."

"Lead with two bombs, and rockets, fuel sweet. We have enough fuel for one more pass on the farmhouse, then we'll start home."

"Lead, you've taken a pot full of hits. You're leaking fuel, and there's smoke coming from your right wing root," Two advised in a high pitch voice.

"Lead, this is Three, jettison all ordnance. There's flames coming from under your engine."

Tommy pulled the lanyard that cleaned the aircraft wings of his bombs and rocket pods. The engine quit. The aircraft dropped like the proverbial crowbar. Flames heated the cockpit. His body sweated profusely and the smoke brought tears to his eyes…it was hot. An electrical fire behind the instrument panel and the arcing flashes aided his decision making. He turned away from the farmhouse and was fortunate to have a plowed field in front of him. This crash was easier on him than the other two because the snow was deeper and his crash landing technique flawless. Experience is the best teacher, he thought. Other than the fire, the aircraft held together fairly well. He exited the blazing plane as it came to a stop and set a record for running in two feet of snow. As he approached the tree line, a voice called out, "Stop, you lucky son of a bitch." Not having any other plan in mind, he stopped.

With his flight circling overhead, he felt almost invincible…even though his 38 caliber snub nose revolver was no match to any soldier with a rifle. Out of the snow, dressed in a dirty white camouflaged coveralls emerged a smiling red-headed paratrooper.

"I'm Sergeant Lee Welch, 101st Airborne pathfinder, and you, Lieutenant "Lucky Ass," just ran through my mine field. I spent all night sliding around on my stomach freezing my nuts off, putting them mines in to trap those two tanks that you fly-boys so ceremoniously tried to dispatched."

Tommy's relief hearing an American voice with a New England twang was immediate but he couldn't keep his mouth from commenting, "Well, Sergeant, I'm sorry we spoiled your surprise party, but there's only one tank and a gasoline truck."

"Bullshit. There were two, one in the barn, and there's a second one in the farmhouse."

"Got a radio, Sergeant?"

"Yes I do."

"Dial in 116.2 and let me talk," Tommy said as the first shell from the remaining tank hit his burning aircraft splattering the "Jug's" wings and tail feathers over the country side.

"Green Flight, Lead here. If you read, second tank is in the farmhouse. Get him before he finds us."

"Green Three reads you five square, and we are in with rockets…and by the by, who is us?" asked Amos Jackson.

Sergeant Welch shook his head. Tommy noting the gesture replied "Just me and a little gray mouse."

Green Three rolled in and fired three five-inch rockets through the glass of the kitchen window, resulting in a tremendous fire ball that marked the end of the second panzer and the farmhouse.

"If your pilots have any rockets left, I have a target that might interest them," Sgt. Welch informed Tommy.

Tommy replied, "Among the three of them, they have 27 five-inch HVAR rockets available."

Welch pointed out on his map a small road a quarter mile away to the north. With his warm breath exhaling a mist of water vapor into the cold air, he said, "The road appears to terminate in a large clump of trees where camouflaged trucks are loading rations and munitions. They arrived last night, and I figure they'll depart tonight. Think your boys can slow down their departure?"

"Hell, they'll do better than that." Into the hand held radio he ordered, "Green Three take up a heading of 280 for two miles from the burning farmhouse and have the flight work over the tree area with their rockets."

Green Three, who was now the flight leader, made his first pass on the trees. "We'll have nothing but kindling wood for a damage assessment but let's humor our grounded leader," he ordered the flight. The first explosion rocked his aircraft. Green Three was glad he didn't press the attack to a lower altitude.

As Green Four rolled in, the camouflage started to burn away, and the pilot blurted out over the radio, "Sweet Jesus, there's at least 20 two-and-a-half-ton trucks parked there." He made the first of three passes. What the five-inch rockets didn't destroy, the secondary explosions did.

"Sarge, how long have you been out here?" asked Tommy.

"Almost a week. We're looking for the main line of resistance but have only found small splinter groups that intend to slow our forces down. If your troops still have any ammo left and want a nice little target, there's couple of observation planes parked in a tunnel two miles northeast of here." He pointed to a red dot on his map that showed a highway tunnel next to a rail siding. Tommy noted several more red dots on his paper.

Tommy grabbed the radio. "Green Flight take up a heading 345 degrees for two miles and look for a tunnel next to a rail siding. Two observation aircraft parked inside. Acknowledge?"

"Green Flight's en-route. That little gray mouse sure knows where all the cheese is hidden," came the answer from Green Three's pilot.

"Green flight this is not going to be a piece of cake," admitted Green Three after his first pass on the tunnel. Although there wasn't any ground fire, the target became a challenge because of the mountain the tunnel was dug into.

"This is like trying to hit the bull's eye on the dart board," Green Four, one of the new pilots in the squadron replied, as he damn near mushed into the mountainside pressing the attack. Full power with his turbocharger blowing saved his ass, but a brown spot showed up on his shorts. The new pilot watched as Green Two eventually put a rocket in the tunnel. Green Two had his P-47 on the deck when he fired, and the rocket hit the ground flat and lazily sailed into the parked aircraft. The debris came flying out of the tunnel, and although he wasn't knocked out of the sky, his armored plating took a beating. "My bank shot was pretty effective," a wise cracking Green Two transmitted.

"Your bank shot could have blown up in your face," Green Three replied.

"*Sour grapes*," from Bartholomew.

"Green One, we are bingo on fuel and have a little battle damage. We're heading for home. What's your plan?" asked Green Three.

Tommy looked at the sergeant and asked, "Do you want to get rid of some of those red dots?"

Welch nodded.

"Green Three, I'll stay with the mouse who promises more cheese tomorrow. Call me on tactical frequency seven at first light. We'll be in the neighborhood." Our call sign will be Gray Mouse," radioed Tommy as he winked at his source of target information.

The wind blowing through the pine trees seemed to increase as the flight departed sending a cold blast of mixed snow and ice crystals at Tommy's face. In the excitement, he hadn't thought about the snow, but at this moment, he knew it would be a problem keeping warm. Welch revealed his plan which encompassed a solution to his problem. "We need to be five miles northeast of here by midnight in order to meet with five others in my stick… that's what we paratroopers call our small units. We have time to strip some clothes for you off the Germans your buddies stopped. Follow me, and step only in my footsteps. My mine field begins where your airplane initially hit the ground. You are one lucky son of a bitch," he chuckled.

"Could you call me Lieutenant or sir or Tommy? I know this is your playground, but I really dislike being called a son of a bitch, lucky or otherwise."

"You got it, Lieutenant. Try to keep up."

They traversed the mine field in silence, not really out of respect for the dead, but with ears tuned in for any sound that would give away a third-party's presence. They heard air escaping from the body of the man Tommy stripped of his fur-lined jacket and light gray coveralls. The sound sent shivers up his back. He also confiscated the dead man's MP40 machine gun and extra bullets.

"Okay, Lieutenant, let's swing by the farmhouse and see if there's any food left in the cellar." Tommy had no problem keeping up. They removed the debris from over the burned storm door to the cellar, and were rewarded with two small hams and three jars of jelly. After a ten-minute break, the trek to meet the other five paratroopers in Welch's stick began.

Chapter 16

Only once did this couple, during their zigzag trip, come close to any German troops. Crossing the road leading to the tunnel where the observation planes had been destroyed, a convoy of six trucks with troops passed within six yards of their position as they hid under a scrub pine. In the fading light, Welch made another red dot next to the red dot he had crossed out. He whispered, "We'll come back later."

Keeping to the shadows, in and out of the tree line, sometimes crawling on their hands and knees, frequently slithering on their stomachs, and on occasion walking upright, they arrived at a rise that overlooked the town of Bullingen, Belgium. The town's lights were out, and only a few campfires were seen in that black inkwell that surrounded the settlement.

Tommy didn't hear or see anyone approach when Welch knocked the would-be assassin down. In a stage whisper, he said "Stop, he is one of ours!" Only then did

Tommy realize how close he came to having his throat sliced open.

"Lucky son of a bitch," the man with the dagger said as he slid it down to a casing on his boot.

"Wilson, he'd rather be called Lieutenant," came a sarcastic reply from Welch. "Tell me what you have."

"Sarge, there's heavy traffic, mostly tanks heading north towards the Eisenborn Ridge. I counted thirty three, but I had to get out of my tree because a patrol was headed my way...my count is probably short," Wilson reported.

To a man, the four other team members told of heavy traffic, mostly tanks, heading in the same direction.

"Damn if you guys haven't described a counter offensive...from the numbers reported, it's going to start in the near future," Tommy interjected.

"Sounds like the lieutenant's a fucking prophet," someone hidden in the black night remarked.

"More like one of those damn desk jockeys from Intel," another chimed in. This one with a decidedly southern drawl.

"Okay, knock it off and follow me," ordered Gray Mouse.

Welch's new plan was to retrace their steps back to the tunnel to determine what activity was taking place that necessitated six trucks of troops. He wanted to be there at sun up. His "move it out" command was met with not a whole hell of a lot of enthusiasm, but his troopers moved

Christmas Help

out like the disciplined warriors they were. Three miles of back-tracking was easy for Tommy because all he had to do was keep up with those who broke trail. The team's movements were choreographed so as to cover and confuse anyone that might stumble upon them. At irregular intervals two team members would head off at a tangent and then circle back to rejoin the stick. Stopping short of the road leading to the tunnel, Welch ordered the men, "Rotate a sentinel and get some rest."

"I'll check on the situation up at the tunnel," he advised the crew as he melted into the blackness. Whatever rotation was decided on took ten seconds, and in another ten seconds, the other three appeared to be sound asleep. Tommy's sleep came and went as his body got cold and then warm as he remembered the blazing fire at the honeymoon cabin. He was in the middle of a sweet dream about Peggy when a cold hand went over his mouth and a menacing Welch whispered, "When's your birthday, Lieutenant?"

"Next month on the thirteenth," answered a groggy Thompson.

"Hell, I was hoping it was today because I have a neat present for you." As the other five gathered around under the tree, he continued, "The trucks are parked next to the railroad siding, and it appears the troops are on their way to the farmhouse. There are three guards, two of them asleep, babysitting a German observation aircraft sitting on the road under the trees. Don't know what it's called, but it is a tail-dragger with a high wing and long landing gear."

"Sounds like a Storch. Some people call it "Stork," ventured Tommy.

"Whatever it is, it's yours and your ride home if no one shoots you down. You do seem prone to having your ass blown out of the sky. Do you want to give it a try?"

"How about doing it now, and I'll loiter around and wait for the fighters to show and they can escort me home. As I recall, there's room for at least one more man, maybe two. Any takers?

Welch rubbed his chin and said, "Take Sergeant Wilson. He'll have all the information we have gathered, and he can present it to the "wheels" without saying fuck every other word."

"Do I have to, Lee? You know I don't mind jumping out of airplanes. It's the landings that scare the shit out of me."

"You'll get in that airplane with the lieutenant and stay in it until it lands and then give your report. Then you may have a drink for each one of us. The lieutenant will buy them."

A few more details were exchanged between Tommy and Welch, then the pathfinders formulated their plan. "Follow me, Lieutenant," commanded Welch.

As the paratroopers approached to within 100 feet of the aircraft, the guards were awake and stomping the snow off their boots. One man started to climb into the cockpit and Welch took aim. Tommy nudged him and said, "Let him get it started." Welch nodded his approval.

"Wilson, take three and stay to the left… between the aircraft and the two guards. When the motor is running good, put them down. I'll get whoever is in the cockpit from the left side, and, Lieutenant, you climb up on the right to take control of the aircraft. I won't be shooting, so don't worry about dodging bullets."

The plan was simplicity at its best. Better yet, it worked. After Wilson's team took care of the two guards, he helped Welch dump the German pilot out of the aircraft.

"Hey Lee, do you want your pig sticker?" yelled Wilson. It had fallen out of the man's throat during the dumping.

"You bet your sweet ass I do. Throw it down and get this thing in the air." Wilson expertly threw it down sticking it in the corpse's back.

"Show off," said a grinning Welch.

Chapter 17

Pouring the coal to that "Storch" was a rather large mistake in that it nearly swapped ends. Airborne in less than 200 feet and climbing like a homesick angel, Tommy finally managed to exercise some control over the aircraft. Leveling the aircraft at 400 feet, he flew a left rectangular pattern to avoid the area around the farmhouse. He was able to try a few basic maneuvers in preparation for the landing at his home base, but the damn thing wouldn't stall. His passenger finally said, "Lieutenant, if that's the best you can do to keep this thing straight and level, then let me out and I'll walk back."

"Aren't you the one that almost slit my throat? Well, paybacks are hell. See if you can get that radio working and if it can tune to 118.3."

Wilson found a headset that almost fit and, with a little bit of luck, was able to tell Tommy, "There's someone on this frequency telling Green Flight to check in."

Elated with Wilson's good fortune with the radio, Tommy tried transmitting but had no luck in receiving an answer. "Move some of the switches. We must be on intercom," Tommy said as he had visions of Green Flight pouncing on his aircraft and blasting him into the next world.

"Green Flight, this is Tommy, do you read me?"

"This is Green One with all aircraft on this frequency. Who the hell is Tommy?"

Damn it, Major Peck is leading the flight and my vision of this aircraft being blown out of the early morning sky is all of a sudden quite clear. Tommy transmitted, "I'm Thompson…Gray Mouse's airborne eyes, and I'm in a German observation aircraft called a Storch. I'm left of your rendezvous point at 300 feet. Gray Mouse has two quick targets for you, but I need an escort back home. My fuel may be critical, but I'm not sure."

"Tommy I don't know how the hell you got that airplane but Green Three and Four will escort you home. What's your maximum speed?"

"The needle hasn't gone past ninety knots. I'll climb to a thousand feet, where I can maintain a visual on your flight."

"Three has a tallyho, and we'll try to join after we drop our bombs."

The trip home lasted one hour. That sixty minutes was filled with smart-ass remarks concerning the lack of airspeed on Tommy's part and nasty quips about ham-fisted fighter pilots who couldn't hold formation on their leader.

"Tower, this is Green Three, inbound at 1,000 feet

three miles north, escorting a German observation aircraft piloted by one of our pilots. Advise our anti-aircraft crews if they put one hole in that aircraft, we will take it as an insult and retaliate."

"Green Three, we understand. Have the pilot park in the infield with his aircraft shut down and his hands where the Military Police can see them."

It was like landing an elevator. A pasty face Wilson looked at Tommy and remarked "That was more of a coming together of earth and aircraft than a landing. My hands are out the window and I don't like looking at the business end of that .50 caliber." When ordered to exit, they did so by the rules outlined in the regulations. They came to a position of attention when a general officer moved in front of them.

"Name, rank, and organization, if you please, gentlemen," the voice demanded from below a pair of icy black eyes.

"Thompson, T.C., First Lieutenant , 363rd Fighter Group, General."

"Wilson, Gerald G., Staff Sergeant, 101st Airborne, Pathfinders, General."

"Thompson, is that your blood on that jacket?" queried the general.

"No sir. The blood belongs to the former occupant, a German foot soldier."

"Take it off and you two follow me," the one-star suggested as he quick step off towards his staff car.

Chapter 18

Beaming with delight, the general's staff couldn't believe the information that Wilson briefed them on. Tommy was amazed that Wilson had not said fuck one time.

"I want this mission worked up for the earliest execution. You two, Thompson and Wilson, follow me," the general ordered.

He led his small expedition over to brief the 101st Airborne Commander, who became more than a little pissed off because he wasn't included in on the initial briefing. In a huffy voice he reminded Wilson, "You belong to me, body and soul. Loyalty," he roared, "to your unit and commander is paramount. Having said that, nice work Sergeant." After the two generals simmered down, the group returned to the conference room, where the weather officer threw in the present and forecasted outlook for the Eisenborn area, which in Thompson's fighter pilot vocabulary equated to "dog shit."

The generals left the room, and the staff went on a tirade of "if only," "need more time," and became prophets of doom and destruction. Staff Sergeant Wilson's subtle suggestion of, "I could parachute in with a Eureka homing beacon, and our stick could set it up for the fighters' advantage. We can position the device within a reasonable distance to the enemy tanks so that your pilots wouldn't be dropping blind."

"Sounds too iffy dropping you through the clouds," noted one colonel.

"I could take him in the same way I brought him out," Tommy said before he thought of the consequences.

"I would rather parachute in during the dark of night than ride that fucking oversized mosquito again," objected Wilson.

"At least you waited until the briefings were finished before you said fuck," whispered Tommy.

The generals arrived back in the room with the aroma of bourbon floating in the air around them. They listened to the "broad-brush" picture, nodded their approval, and the plan was set in motion to be executed the next morning.

That evening at the Augur Inn, as suggested by Sgt. Welch, Tommy had six shots of Old Turkey lined up in front of Wilson.

"Here's to Sergeant Welch," he toasted as he downed the first tumbler. "Here's to Jake, Peter and George," quickly downing the next three. "And here's to Sam," he quietly whispered as he tipped the glass.

"Who's Sam, Sergeant Wilson?"

"Sam was our sixth stick man. Unlucky son of a bitch. His chute didn't open when we jumped in on this mission. Good man, he was."

Tommy drank one in honor of Welch and his comrades, then listen to Green Flight and others sing,

The moonlight shone on the bar room floor,
The place was closed for the night.
When out of the corner
Came a little gray mouse and he sat in the pale moon light.
He lapped up the liquor on the bar room floor
And back on his haunches he sat.
And to that empty room he called
Bring on your God damn cat.

"Lieutenant, are you nuts?" asked Major Peck as he slid his bar stool next to Tommy.

"A little touched in the head, but definitely not nuts. Did you do any good after I left the barn area, sir?"

"We bombed out the trucks and then our strafing passes, combined with the Germans running into the Gray Mouse's mine field, we cleaned out that nest. We bombed two other of Gray Mouse's targets, and then the weather went down to 200 feet with visibility less than a mile. Gray Mouse indicated that his troops were going to rest in the tunnel, and weather permitting, he would contact us at first light. Doesn't look good for flight operations in that area tomorrow due to forecasted bad weather."

"Sir, I need someone to escort me and the sergeant to within five miles of the tunnel and contact Gray Mouse that I'm en route. I'll ask if he can find some flares to shoot when he hears my motor. The visibility is forecast to be less than a half mile in snow showers and I'll need help in locating the team…I would be eternally grateful for any assistance Gray Mouse can give me," begged Tommy.

"Thompson, you really are nuts, but I'll lead you in because we need that homing beacon in place. There some doubt in my mind that you can pull this off but the general said 'it's a go' loud and clear. I'll have maintenance give me a stripped aircraft so I can slow down to enable you to fly on my wing. Take a couple of jerry cans of gas for the trip home. I don't think that the Stork has a range of more than 300 miles. Now get back to tent city and try to get some sleep."

"Yes sir," Tommy said respectfully. That man has some brass balls, he thought as he escorted Wilson to a tent with an extra bed. "I'll wake you at 0400. We'll get a bite to eat and get some food for your stick. Then we'll get reacquainted with the Stork"

"Thanks, Lieutenant," said a slightly tipsy Pathfinder. Both were sound asleep before the clock's hands indicated 1800 hours

As Tommy sat on the side of his bunk he mused, is it my skill and cunning, or is it St. Teresa working overtime? Reacting to this thought process, his guardian angel just smiled to himself and prepared his bag of luck.

Chapter 19

Sergeant Wilson was dressed and on his feet when Tommy awoke. The mess tent was alive with ground crews getting ready to start the day while others were dragging their tired butts in from finishing up the night chores on the flight line.

"Sarge, me and the lieutenant are going back to our buddies behind the lines and need some chow to take to them. Any chance for some cold cuts and cheese?"

The cook looked at Tommy for confirmation. Tommy nodded. The cook rolled his eyes in disbelief then motioned them on. He came over to their table as they were finishing their breakfast of scrambled eggs and chipped beef on toast. Wilson looked up at him and said, "This is the best shit on a shingle I've ever eaten."

"I don't usually get compliments on my "SOS" but I'll take yours without the proverbial grain of salt. Men going behind the lines tend to tell truth before they shove off." He handed them a large box of steaming meat, "Good luck and I'll have some T-bone steaks for you and your crew when you get back." He gave them a heavy pat on their backs and left for the serving line.

"You got a great outfit, Lieutenant," said Wilson. "There are some cooks who would have told me to piss up a rope. If I could ever get used to landing, I might consider re-enlisting with you air corps people. Please don't tell Lee I said that."

Pre-flighting the aircraft was a piece of cake. Starting it, however, required a crew chief who could read the instructions on the placard that were printed in German. Major Peck's aircraft was next to the Stork. The major kept shaking his head in disbelief as he watched this dog-and-pony show as Tommy and the ground crew shouted and pointed instructions to each other. Finally the food, gas, special equipment and crew were in the Stork with the engine running, and after receiving a green light from the tower authorizing his takeoff, Tommy got airborne. Peck waited until it appeared that the Stork was at max speed, then easily joined up on Tommy's left wing. Peck moved forward ever so slowly so Tommy was able to hold a loose right wing position. At 500 feet, they were in milky clouds as smooth as silk for their flight of an hour and five minutes. Not a word was spoken for the hundred and ten mile leg. Peck pointed at Tommy, then toward the ground and the P-47 disappeared as the two aircraft separated.

"Gray Mouse, this is Green One. Your stick member is being delivered in the same way he left. If you can, could you use a light, flare, or smoke to guide him in. Do it when you hear my engine. Do you copy?"

"Green One, I copy and can do. I hear your motor. Your man is nuts."

"Gray Mouse, this is Lieutenant Lucky Ass and I am only half as nuts as your crew."

Tommy's letdown from the clouds went well, but at 300 feet, still in and out of the murk. Dropping to 200 feet, he asked Wilson what he could see.

"Snowflakes," came a hurried reply. "Wait a second. Over to the left there is a fire. Looks like they're burning one of the Kraut's trucks."

"I see it. Hang on Wilson, this might be a little hairy," Tommy warned as he stood the aircraft on its left wing momentarily. Then, with a ninety degree banking turn to the right, he had the aircraft lined up with a snow-covered road leading into the tunnel. Again the landing was an arrival and the landing roll less than 100 feet.

"Lieutenant, with another four or five landings, you might get the hang of this critter, but by God, I don't intend to be with you," a sweating Wilson remarked. Members of the stick came up, and Wilson handed down the homing equipment, gas, and food. He supervised loading the gas, which was not an easy task with the engine running, but most of it went into the tank. Sergeant Welch, now known as "Gray Mouse," leaned into the cockpit with Tommy who asked, "Could you place that homing device within a mile of the tank concentration?"

"Might take two or three days, but you can count on it. Weather is pretty lousy for you fly boys. Tell your guys to get their gonads up cause it's not going to be a picnic for us ground troops either," was his reply. They shook hands.

The men picked up the Stork's tail and turned the aircraft around. "Green One, Gray Mouse Eyes airborne, heading home, package delivered. I'll stay at 500 feet for an hour and then let down to 200 feet for the rest of the flight."

"Green One copies. I'll notify tower of your intentions. Good show…Lieutenant Lucky Ass indeed. I'll see you back at the Auger Inn. I'm buying."

Tommy's landing turned out to be the best he made in the Stork. "It's too bad Wilson isn't here to witness this rare feat," he said to his empty aircraft. Again the military police surrounded the aircraft and Tommy again assumed the position of surrender.

Chapter 20

"Amos do you think this freezing drizzle, snow and fog will ever lift? This lousy weather has kept the Luftwaffe and us growing roots."

"While we're sitting here, the German offensive has pretty much surrounded the allied troops in and around Bastogne. Casualties are high as the enemy cannons are relentlessly pounding perimeter defenses and then followed up with infantry surges. Damn it Tommy, we could really do some good if we ever get airborne. If we don't get into this fray pretty soon they're going to either run us over or pushed back the allies… hell maybe all the way to France."

In desperation, the wing commander ordered the all three chaplains confined in the chapel. "You three are supposed to have an inside track to the Almighty. Well get cracking and pray for good weather and don't stop until the sun shines."

After three days, the weather lifted enough for the C-47's to start supplying the troops with ammunitions, food and replacements. An aggressive campaign with C-47's towing gliders through a sky full of flak enabled the American troops to barely hold on to the city of Bastogne by their fingertips. The campaign was successful in re-supplying, but at a terrible cost of gliders, C-47s and crews. The westward advance of the Germans slowed but not stopped.

Leading the third flight of a 20-ship raid, Tommy's Green Flight of four was circling above a small break in the clouds. The Eureka homing beacon planted by Sgt. Welch's stick enabled the fighters to locate and engage the enemy. Calmly waiting his flight's turn, he listened to the preceding flights comments on weather, targets and flak.

"White one…I broke out at 500 feet above the ground…visibility is about two miles…and the flak is thick as flies on cow dung…keep it moving…tanks on both sides of the road."

"White two…I'm getting hammered…pulling up…meet you on top."

Leading his flight into this quagmire of guns reminded him of the sick joke where men on a desolate island rid themselves of their pent up sexual drive by inserting their erections into the cork hole of a barrel where one of the men serviced the others. "Looks like its my turn in the barrel," he quietly reminded himself. Bartholomew chuckled at the remembrance of that nasty but titillating anecdote.

"Green Flight, rockets first then napalm. Dropping those canisters is going to be dicey…drop them as you pull up…one pass and then we haul ass," Tommy instructed the members of his flight.

"Green Two, roger."

"Green Three, roger."

"Green Four, roger."

Later at debriefing, Green Three, Amos Jackson, reluctantly confirmed Green Two's account, "Tommy had salvoes his rockets and released his napalm at a nest of "triple A" which he knocked out, but not before they hosed him. He was streaming smoke on his pull-up, never said a word and we never saw him again."

What really happened was that Tommy, nursing his wounded aircraft, couldn't get enough altitude to bail out. I'm headed towards Bastogne…not positive that this is a good idea, but under the circumstances I don't have much choice. Whoa what's that! A hellacious loud backfire, followed by a wimpy sputter, announced the stoppage of his propeller. Not again, he thought. He dropped out of the cloud and spotted a cemetery off to his left. Several glider aircraft were on the ground next to it, some intact but most were in pieces scattered about the snow-covered field. His aircraft slid into a wrecked glider showering his burning P-47 with plywood. His dismount wasn't exactly graceful but the flames that licked around his cockpit were toasting his buns, He started to run for cover among the headstones when he heard a familiar voice yell, "Stop, you lucky son of a bitch, Lieutenant, sir."

"You know, we can't keep meeting like this. People will start to talk," a grinning Welch chuckled.

Sergeant Wilson remarked to Tommy "You don't have that landing thing down yet, sir." Pointing to the burning aircraft, one of the team members asked, "Lieutenant, did you bring any marshmallows?"

Happy to be alive and among friends, Tommy shot back, "Men, I have news from the front…we're winning." His humor was rewarded with a snowball to the side of his head and the landing of three artillery rounds 100 yards away.

Ducking behind the tombstones, Welch informed him, "We're being chased by six SS Troops as we entered this cemetery. There's lots of good cover among the stones. We need to get back to our platoon who are on the west side of this bone yard. If you can carry some of the supplies we emptied out of that glider you ran into, it will free another one of us to slow down those SS Troopers, who by the way haven't taken a liking to us."

"Give me what you want…I have so much adrenalin pumping, I can probably carry two loads," boasted Tommy.

"Don't let your mouth overload your ass, Lieutenant. This graveyard is over a mile wide. And our handicap is six Germans, who are fair to middling shooters. Wilson, go fifteen yards and then cover me as I come up. Try not to lose the lieutenant. He brought us chow when we needed it, and he'll be carrying rations for the platoon. If I can knock one of them down, then we'll try twenty yards next. Stay low and get moving."

The first fifteen yards yielded one German trooper, who, for whatever reason, stood up partially shielded by a statue of an angel, her arms reaching down as if to embrace him. As the trooper fell, he grabbed an arm and pulled the statue down on top of him. The kiss she planted on his forehead was the kiss of death.

Welch caught up to the group with a new plan. "Lieutenant, drop those supplies and then get ready to dash for that statue of the holy family. Wilson, take George and cover two rows down to the left, and I'll take Peter and Jake and cover this position and the right flank. Any Questions? Good. Lieutenant, move out."

Here I am, bait again, thought Tommy, his heart pumping in time with one of Gene Krupa's solo drum beats. He zigzagged for the safety of the holy family. A bullet ricocheted off Edith Rumlace's tombstone as he dashed by it, another bounced off Edith's mother and father's memorial as he continued to run through the ornamental markers. Another bullet scored a direct hit on the ceramic portrait of her husband as a stumbling Tommy threw himself at the feet of the holy family statue, and prayed, "Mary, I hope this robe I'm touching is marble and not real cloth because I'm not ready to be in your presence."

Bartholomew's thought was, *this kid must have a death wish that I wasn't informed about. He keeps volunteering.*

A volley of gun fire followed, none of which was aimed at Tommy. A silence fell over this final resting place as five more German warriors were welcomed to their destiny.

"Lieutenant, come on back and pick up the supplies," called Welch. "We can get on with our journey, and thanks for volunteering to be the rabbit. My men are better shooters than runners."

"Did anyone see me raise my hand? I sure as hell didn't. And you're welcome," Thompson grumbled as he easily lifted the cartons of rations. Tommy felt his heart pounding against his chest as the thought of what he had done was pushed to the back of his mind. Bartholomew breathed a sigh of relief thinking, *this kid will try anything.*

At the town's defensive perimeter, Sergeant Welch introduced Tommy to his captain. "Always glad to have another platoon leader on our team, Lieutenant."

"I'm not infantry, sir. I'm a pilot," Tommy informed him.

"You're a commissioned officer in the United States Army, and you are a platoon leader until you find an airplane to fly out of here. Lee, he's your leader… take good care of him. He's a little green and the green ones don't last too long."

"Yes, sir. Lieutenant, follow me to your home away from home."

Chapter 21

"What do you mean another birthday present?" exclaimed the new platoon leader, blowing his warm breath on his freezing fingers. No campfires were allowed to ward off the chill of winter's harsh wind blowing through the war torn town of Bastogne.

Welch explained through chattering teeth, "I found it after our last patrol. The one where your brilliant plan led us into an ambush with an enemy patrol… two of our new men became part of the walking wounded. I don't know how you got out of that mess without a scratch. Later that evening you led us into a snarling pack of dogs, resulting in my ass getting bitten by some damn German shepherd. I can't get over that my first wound in combat came from some damn mutt. Wilson, quit that snickering. Any way I went back to the barn to see what the dogs were protecting. To make a long story short, there was this dead old man leaning against the tire of this two-wing aircraft. He had on a bright red flight suit with a long white scarf around his neck. Maybe he was going for a spin around the town…hell, who knows what he had planned? Guess his heart wasn't up to it. Anyway, the aircraft looks like it's in good shape, but what the hell do I know about airplanes? Want to take a look see?"

"Sergeant Welch, you're not trying to get rid of your reluctant leader, are you? And what about the dogs?" asked Tommy warming up to the prospect of an airplane to fly.

"The truth is, sir, you're too damn fearless for us ordinary mortals. We've been on the ground end of this war since we jumped in at Normandy, and we would like to be celebrating in Berlin at the end of the war. I think we can reach that goal with you in the blue and away from us. And those starving dogs are with their master," a straight-faced Welch replied.

At the barn, Tommy marveled at the sight of the shiniest, most beautiful biplane he had ever seen. "Although the plane had Belgium markings, the placards are in English, and if I remember correctly, this is a Hawker Fury made by the British. I saw a Movietone news reel showing nine of this type aircraft with their wingtips literally tied together before they split into three flights of three and put on an amazing air show back in the early '30s. I think our departed old gentleman was an acrobatic pilot who wanted one more thrill, regardless of the risks of flying in a flak-saturated sky." Tommy's joy was difficult to hide as his hand stroked the shiny fuselage in a manner reserved for a loved one.

"What are the chances that the captain will let me try to fly out of this mess?" asked Tommy to no one in particular.

"It's a done deal, Lieutenant. I volunteered our platoon to cover the northern sector where casualties have been a little high…"

"A little high, my ass! The last three platoons were pretty much wiped out," interrupted Wilson.

Silencing Wilson with a dirty look, Welch continued, "As I was saying, Lieutenant, we traded you for the assignment. When do you want to leave?"

"Soon as we can get some snow off the ground for a take off run and I spend some time looking over this beauty," answered Tommy with enthusiasm.

"Jake, take the tractor with the blade attachment and run it straight from the barn doors for a thousand feet. The ground is frozen solid, so make your run as smooth as you can," ordered Welch.

After taking off on the icy, make-shift runway, Tommy listened to the Rolls-Royce V-12 engine purring like a contented kitten as he headed north to look over his platoon's newly assigned area. He made a couple 360-degree turns at low altitude over the startled German troops who took some pot shots at his red menace. He heard the pinging as some of the bullets struck the aircraft, and then headed back to the barn. The landing was a little dicey but he was able to bring it to a stop, even though the braking action was almost nil, just inside the barn.

Shaking his head, Welch raced forward, put his hands on his hips and yelled, "You have had that airplane for ten minutes, and already you got three holes in the tail. Why are you back here?"

Tommy smiled and shouted, "That trap you were heading to can be defeated by sliding your troops east 400 yards and circle back. There's a thick cover of trees on a slight rise that will conceal your movements. They have their mortars set up at the rear with very little protection. Good luck. Now push me around, and I'll get out of your hair."

After the aircraft was turned, the men lined up, came to the position of attention and gave "their" lieutenant the smartest salute they had given any one since D Day. Tommy returned the salute, advanced the throttle and was airborne again, heading south.

The aircraft handled beautifully, and Tommy couldn't resist doing barrel rolls, inverted flight and even a loop or two. He encountered no resistance, until he came to his own air base. The triple A forced him back. He spotted a flight of four P-47's about to enter the landing pattern and decided to join them. He approached them from the rear and low and muscled his aircraft in between the leader and his element.

"Red Lead, Red Three here, there's some nut in a bi-wing trying to take my place in the formation. Hell, he just did. Do you want me to ram him?"

"Red Lead, Red Two here… the pilot looks a lot like Thompson…only dirtier and needs a shave."

"Red Flight, let's not bend any aircraft...hold him in there tight and we'll let the ground cops take care of him. Tower, Red Flight on initial with five for landing."

There was some mild bouncing up and down from the P-47's but Tommy held his position on the Red Two right through the landing and taxi back to the squadron area. He shut the engine down and assumed the surrender position before the military police surrounded him.

Amos was in the entourage that met the prostrate intruder. "Damn it, Tommy. You missed your memorial service this morning. It really was beautiful. Especially the eulogy, which I gave with all the conviction of a repented sinner. The choir sang the Army Air Corps song and that line when they sing, 'we live in fame or go down in flames,' well it almost brought a tear to my eye. Then the bugler played taps outside the chapel and, believe it or not, it sounded as if the notes were coming from another world. And all those prayers from the brass down to the junior latrine keeper...all those prayers... were wasted," exclaimed Amos Jackson. "Tommy it was just fucking beautiful. Too bad you missed it." He gave Tommy a bear hug and stammered, "At least I don't have to inventory all your shit."

"Excuse me, lieutenants. The commander wants to see both of you," the ranking military policeman said, a little bit annoyed that this same intruder kept bringing in these foreign aircraft here without permission. It made him uncomfortable seeing these officers hug each other like they were fairies.

"Keep an eye on my birthday present, sergeant. It's a pretty little rascal and has just a few holes in the tail," Tommy shouted over his shoulder as they hurried him off.

"And who in the hell gave you this birthday present?" a half smiling Major Peck asked.

"Sir, it came from our friend Gray Mouse, who seems to have a knack for finding these types of trophies."

"And where did you run into Gray Mouse?" the major asked scratching his head.

"In the cemetery at Bastogne, where he used me for bait. After they eliminated the six Germans who were chasing us, he introduced me to his company commander, who made me their platoon leader," Tommy was quick to explain. "I did that chore for four days and wasn't very good at it. Gray Mouse got me this birthday present and permission from the company commander to fly away."

"Thompson, go debrief with intelligence and we'll finish up later. I have to cancel that missing-in-action letter I sent to your wife. First Sergeant, see what you can do to stop that letter," he yelled through the open door.

"Yes sir," came as a vocal duet from Tommy and the First Sergeant.

Tommy, with Amos Jackson at his side, went to the debriefing room, while the First Sergeant had his orderly room troops jumping through their assholes looking for the missing in action letter. Private Conway finally spoke up, "Sarge, it's here in my typewriter. I haven't had time to finish it."

"What do you mean you haven't had time to finish it? Isn't there twenty four hours in a day? When I give you a job to do I want it finished yesterday. Give me that damn letter. Why couldn't you finish it Conway?" he bellowed as he ripped the letter into small pieces.

"You put me on the Kitchen Police roster three days ago and I got off this morning," Conway replied, stepping back awaiting the first soldier's wrath.

"Well, wasn't that smart of me to foresee the need to not send this letter by sending your ass to K.P. duty. Next time Conway, finish the damn job."

Chapter 22

"Peggy sweetheart, you've been pretty quiet these last couple of days. I know you miss Tommy and so do your father and I. This New Year's Eve party won't be a happy occasion but for the sake of the other families in the parish put a smile on your face."

"Mom, this two-week semester break has allowed me to catch up with the news from my high school classmates…all thirty-two of them. At our reunion in the church's basement just before Christmas, I learned that all twelve boys from our class had enlisted upon graduation. Now all are in the European theatre of operations. I guess after three months on the front lines they're considered battle-hardened veterans."

"Honey," interjected her dad, "The artillery barrage laid down by the Germans at Bastogne didn't differentiate between veterans and rookies. Two of our town's mothers changed their blue star window flags to ones with gold stars this Christmas. Two others moms' received letters stating that their sons' wounds were being treated and they were receiving the best possible care."

Mary continued, "On the day their sons lay dying or wounded, crying out in agony, their mothers told me they knew their sons were calling out for them. Tears flooded their eyes as their husbands tried to console them saying, 'He's all right, he's fine,' but those mommas knew their sons on a level that no one can explain."

As the church bell rang in the New Year, Peggy's tears splashed on Tommy's tiger photograph. She had read his last letter for the eighth time and prayed that he was safe from the dangers that came from being in that war torn sky. And there were times such as now that she had to convince herself that he was all right and he was safe.

Her prayers seemed to go unnoticed as Tommy and other pilots, ground crews, cooks, bakers and staff "wienies" scrambled to bomb shelters, trenches and even into deep, waste-water pools for protection against the bombing and strafing by the Luftwaffe. Throughout Belgium, Holland, and France, a massive raid by over 900 German aircraft, mostly fighters and fighter bombers, was launched against seventeen Allied air bases. Only a handful of P-47's from Tommy's airfield at Deux Jumeaux, France were able to get airborne, but Tommy did not happen to be one of them. The raid by the Me 109's and FW 109's lasted less than a half hour, but the damage they inflicted was significant.

During those thirty minutes, Tommy's refuge was behind some sandbags which surrounded an antiaircraft gun. He was amazed at the accuracy of the crew as they poured lead from their quad 50 caliber machine guns. This effectiveness stopped when shrapnel from a 20 millimeter cannon burst from a Me 109 wounded one of the gun's crew.

"You there, help me remove the wounded guy from his station." Tommy shouted to the others seeking shelter by the sandbags. Blood was squirting from the man's leg as Tommy's command roared over the explosions of the aircraft burning on the field, "Use my scarf to put a tourniquet above the spot that I'm holding."

"Lieutenant I need help with this gun," came a request equal in loudness from the remaining gun crewman. Tommy was pressed into service by Corporal Fogel. His instructions came fast and furious. The yelling and screaming back and forth were simple, instant communication that was effective in getting the gun back into action.

Tommy kept yelling and pointing with his blood covered hand, "more lead...put them in front...now you got him..." as smoke came out of one of the enemy fighters that had his guns firing into The Auger Inn. "That bastard," Tommy cried out in rage as he watched flames pour out the windows.

"Swing to the left and put it in right in front of the propeller on the son of a bitch pulling up. You got him! Nice shooting. Swing right," an excited and trembling Tommy yelled over the screaming of the Daimler Benz engine in the propeller-less Me 109

"Out of ammo, sir."

"Quick, let's get our asses behind some cover! Nice shooting. What's your name soldier?"

"Corporal Fogel, sir"

"Fogel, it sure got quiet."

They looked to a sky clear of enemy aircraft and then at the field of burning P-47's destroyed or damaged.

"Not any more, sir."

The silence was broken as aircraft fuel cells exploded, spraying aviation gas over adjacent aircraft. Fifty caliber ammunition heated and cooked off, sending bullets into other aircraft far across the field. The damage was spreading rapidly.

"Fogel, let's get your buddy to the medics. Help me lift him. Damn it! You're wounded too. Why didn't you say something?"

"I guess I was too excited."

"You should be excited. Another couple of inches higher and you would have lost half your dick."

"Hell, I thought that wet feeling was from me pissing in my pants, sir."

"Hey, you behind the sand bags, we need some help. You men carry the one with the bad leg wound." Unsure that the action was over, the men at first were slow in reacting. "Damn it, get your ass in gear and tend to this man." Placing his shoulder under the corporal's arm he asked, "Can you walk with me, Fogel?"

"Yes sir, I can, sir." One hundred agonizing pain filled yards later, a second lieutenant, driving one of the triple A's battery's vehicles, pulled up and assisted in getting the men on board. Tommy introduced himself. Reading the man's name stenciled on his field jacket, he continued, "Lieutenant Butts, this man Fogel shot down two Me 109's after he was wounded. I'm recommending a valor award for Corporal Fogel. When that paper work gets to your office I expect your concurrence."

"Sir, my men don't usually get any recognition for their efforts. The ones like Fogel usually end up with personnel folder filled with article fifteen's. He has had his stripes taken away so many times we should put zippers on them. Maybe this will mature him. You just don't know where your heroes come from, do you? Sir, you can bet your last dollar I'll bump your recommendation up the line. For one of my men to receive a decoration will bring recognition to our unit even if he is a troublemaker like Fogel."

Walking a safe distance around the burning aircraft on his way back to his squadron area, Tommy was delighted to see in the midst of the smoke and flames, his latest birthday present. The air had an acrid smell and a bitter taste to it. Oily soot was settling on him, forcing him to put a handkerchief across his face in order to filter the saturated air. The flames reflected off the Fury's shining cowl, and for a moment, Tommy thought it had escaped the assault from above. But in one split second the fuel tanks caught fire, there was a blinding flash, and then it was gone. It disappeared. The heat and smoke rolled over him, smearing oily soot on his already blood stained flight suit. He stood bewildered and perplexed, wondering what else can go wrong. "Damn it," he yelled to no one in particular, "I really liked that birthday present."

Don't get too attached to things, Tommy. Things really have no value in God's eyes. The only creations that have any worth are people, Bartholomew reminded him.

Tommy jogged back to his unit. In the midst of all the confusion in the orderly room caused by the air raid, his entrance caused no one to notice him. He sat down at an Underwood typewriter, dusted it off, and began to slowly type with his blood stained fingers the following: Recommendation for the award of the Bronze Star with a "V" for valor device to Corporal Timothy Fogel, 756th Anti-Aircraft Squadron…A hand touched his shoulder and Private First Class Michael Scott said, "Lieutenant, that's my job. Give me the details, and I will flesh it in…whoa, you're doing this for a corporal? Hell, I'll hand-carry this to his unit when I finish it. Wow! Shot down two Me 109's. No shit…I mean, no shit, sir! And he was wounded!? Damn, I'll drop it off, then go to the hospital and shake that man's hand. Wow, two Me 109's! Hot damn!"

"Scott, make sure you hand that recommendation to Lieutenant Butts. He promised he would push it up the chain of command. And, thanks, I would have been all day two finger typing that recommendation."

Chapter 23

The early morning intelligence briefing given by Lt. Col. Paul Douglas, in the smoke filled squadron operation room bordered on contemptible. "Gentlemen, the following is an interim update on the New Year's day raid on our base. We lost a total of 465 allied fighters, the majority of which were lost on the ground. The Luftwaffe lost 304 aircraft. 277 were downed by allied fighters and the rest by intense anti-aircraft fire. Although we lost more aircraft, the Germans lost 238 pilots who were killed, captured or missing. They might be able to replace those aircraft but not their experienced pilots. We don't know why they risked their pilots for a short-term gain, but we suspect Herman Goring's finger was in this pie. Our replacement aircraft are in Paris at the Aeroport de Paris-Roissy and the C-47 to take you there is awaiting your boarding. Dismissed."

Nervously squirming in the back of a Gooney Bird, a dozen P-47 pilots, notoriously the world's worst passengers, were being bounced around like ping-pong balls due to the rough weather and the aircraft commander playfully yawing the war-weary flying machine. They tried their best to avoid looking at the topless 55 gallon empty barrel that had been tied to the floor. It soon became the gathering place for all those who had breakfast that morning.

Tommy sat with his eyes closed and seemed to be immune to the retching and foul smell, that is, until the man next to him puked in his lap. Tommy took one look at the sticky warm mess then joined the breakfast club at the barrel.

After landing, a grinning aircraft commander watched the pasty face "tigers" deplane and whispered to his co-pilot, "These pussy cats won't be terrorizing the female population of the now Free France capital city of Paris tonight."

Bartholomew snickered at that remark, thinking, *that sounds like a multi-engine pilot's opinion of fighter pilots.*

How wrong the aircraft commander's comments turned out to be. As the sun's last rays disappeared behind the security fence, a stolen truck was making its way towards where ever the music and women gathered. On board were eleven fighter pilots. A little green around the gills but all with a desire that eased their upset stomachs. They left Tommy at the barracks still puking while he tried to wash the smell off his tunic and pants.

Tommy's words of advice to his squadron mates as they departed were, "You are going into a city renowned for its beautiful women, who are reputed to be amazing lovers. In an effort to uphold our image as incredible American studs, try to find women with small hands... they will make your dicks look bigger."

Shortly after two in the morning, his squadron mates, escorted by the military police, staggered back to barracks. The old smell was replaced with the new smell as two of the pilots spent the night hugging the commode.

A bright sun glistened off row after row of P-47's at the marshalling airbase, Aeroport de Paris. On this Valentine's Day in 1945, Tommy would lead three flights of four back to their home base. His remarks during the pre-flight briefing included, "Our call signs will be Wonderful one through twelve. Make your engine checks according to the book. These aircraft may be new but they've been sitting on the ground a long time. Once we get airborne, fly a loose tactical formation in order to discover any problems with these factory-fresh aircraft. I suggest a short inverted flight with a negative "G" in hopes of getting all the loose nuts, bolts and small tools off the floor. Capture those objects that are against the canopy and put them in your pocket. Turn your oxygen regulator to the 100 percent position... maybe the pure air will clear away the cob webs in your brains. After the checks, join in close formation and look sharp as we will be bidding farewell to all those women who are crying their hearts out for their short dick American lovers."

Thirty minutes later, Tommy brought the group on a rather low pass over Paris using the Eiffel Tower as a pylon. "Wonderful flight, you're looking great," Tommy proudly announced.

There wasn't a ripple in the air as they proceeded back to their home base. "Wonderful flight echelon right," was ordered as the aircraft approached their home field. Looking back at his wing men, their canopies were in perfect alignment and not a bounce in the dozen airplanes. As briefed, the flight pitched out in one-second intervals into a tight 360 degree descending turn to land. Taxiing to his parking spot, Tommy couldn't help but wonder if the cut engine signal, a moving hand across the throat, given by the wing commander, was for him or his aircraft's engine. It turned out to be the former.

"Lieutenant Thompson, that was the finest bit of formation flying I've seen since Randolph Field back in 1939. Now with the pleasantries over, the phone call I received from General de Gaulle was two octaves higher than any diva has ever achieved. Even with the poor connection and the language barrier, I could tell he was pissed. Just what in the hell did you do to the Eiffel Tower?"

"Sir, it was just a little formation flyby to salute the Free French," Tommy hesitantly answered.

"Well, I don't buy that hogwash, and tomorrow when you repeat that to the French General, I doubt if he is going to buy it either. Get your cleanest uniform, not the one you're wearing now that smells like puke. Make

Christmas Help

sure you wear all your ribbons, and for Christ sake don't embarrass yourself or this wing more than you already have. The Gooney bird will take you and seven other pilots back to Paris tonight. When that French general gets through eating you a new asshole, your crew will ferry eight more aircraft to Asse, Belgium. Contact your operations officer after you arrive at Asse for the next assignment. And by the way, you were promoted to captain yesterday...I wouldn't get use to wearing those railroad tracks if I were you, because I don't think you're going to keep them very long. Now get out of my sight, Captain. And get your stinking uniform clean."

Chapter 24

A mentally and physically exhausted Captain Tommy C. Thompson squirmed in the outer room of the Commander of the Free French Forces, contemplating his fate. Nervously he pulled at the collar of the too small shirt he borrowed from Amos Jackson. When the general's secretary wasn't looking, Tommy sniffed at his hands, trying to insure that the smell had been washed off with that bar of felsnapta soap. A few beads of sweat careened off his forehead, bounced off his nose and landed squarely on his two rows of decorations.

He could barely hear an aide to the general verbally outlining the new captain's war record to France's soon to be president. "General, he has received awards for valor and gallantry both from his government and the British…"

"And for what event did the British award him a Military Cross, a decoration normally given for a ground combat action?" interrupted the general.

"Sir, at Caen, after he was shot down and wounded, he killed four Germans including one Nazi general officer, which ultimately caused the Germans to abandon their position."

"And what decoration did the French Forces give him?" snapped the general.

"Unfortunately, none, General," the timid reply came from the aide, knowing that the red creeping up on the general's face was a signal to duck.

"This pilot spills his blood on our country's soil, kills a Nazi general officer, wins a battle and we ignore his sacrifice and bravery, and I am scheduled to chastise him for a splendid demonstration of his flying skills? What idiot scheduled this event?" he roared. His next words were too loud and fast to understand as he sprayed spittle across three members of his staff.

Tommy could hear the ranting and raving, but he understood very little of the French language which he tried to learn in high school. He was relieved when ordered into the general's office. He came to the position of rigid attention. And he damn near fell over when the general came up to him, looked him straight in the eye, then bent from his shoulders and kissed him on both cheeks. They stood there at attention as the general's aide in a crisp military voice, read in formal French, from an impressive looking document a citation that ended with the words"…Croix de Guerre." Whereupon, the general pinned a medal on Tommy's chest, kissed him on both cheeks again, stepped back, saluted Tommy, and then exited the room.

The other officers in the room shook his hand and exited through the same door as the general, leaving Tommy alone in the position of attention. Bewildered, Tommy did an about face and left through the door he had entered, thinking, if that was my ass-chewing, I wish our own army would follow the French protocol.

That afternoon, Tommy briefed his crews on the particulars of the flight to Belgium. "I want you all to be in close formation as we pass over the Eiffel Tower. This time we'll be at fifteen hundred feet. I don't think the general would be quite as forgiving as he was this morning if we pressed our luck."

But his actions belied his words as Tommy' flight again roared pass the Eiffel Tower not at fifteen hundred feet but at an altitude where a tower maintenance man was able to looked down at the tops of eight P-47's in perfect formation.

General De Gaulle was admiring the tower from his office window as Tommy's flight swept by and rattled the windows. He shook his head and smiled as he returned Tommy's hand salute. "I remember back in the first war and an insolent, flamboyant American lieutenant fighter pilot who flew upside down over Champs-Elysees…Bartholomew…something or other…he flew with the SPA La Fayette Escadrille," he recalled to his aide.

"*It's nice to be remembered even if it's for my foolish actions,*" thought Bartholomew, airing the rancid smell out of his wings.

"Should I get Thompson's commander on the telephone, General?"

"No, I can't think of a medal that would change Thompson's attitude. Pour me a glass of that Napoleon brandy and let me sit here alone and try to remember the valiant acts of our flyers during the last war."

After landing at the Asse airfield in Belgium, Tommy reported by telephone to his operations officer, "Sir do you have a follow on assignment for us?"

The ops officer's answer surprised him," Bring all the aircraft back home. There was a hell of a lot more damage from the New Year's day air raid than our maintenance team originally estimated. By the by, Captain, how good was the general at chewing out American tush?"

"To tell the truth sir, it was a very pleasant occasion… he even kissed me on the cheeks a couple times," admitted Tommy.

"Don't try to gloss this over. The Wing Commander wants a blow by blow account," the ops officer's voice was starting to sharpen.

"Then I guess you won't believe he pinned the Croix de Guerre on my tunic," Tommy added hesitantly.

"You're right. I don't believe you, Thompson," he screamed. "After you land back here, report to my office. Try not to get shot down on the way home because the wing commander, squadron commander and I have plans for you and we want your butt in one piece."

He really did try hard not to get shot down, but his formation was diverted to troops in contact with the enemy as elements of the U.S. Third Army approached the Rhine River. When supporting ground troops in contact with the enemy, Tommy forgot all restrictions placed on him. He had read in the Stars and Stripes that the German high command, on orders from Hitler, did not want the allies to land on German soil and placed several divisions on the east side of the river with orders to die rather than retreat.

"Green flight, check the truck traffic in our two o'clock position. Looks like they are backed up over a mile about 400 yards from that blown-up bridge. Gentlemen, on the other side of the Rhine River is Germany. That water is moving fast, so if you're unlucky and get shot down, avoid the river… your parachute will drag you down."

"Lead, is it okay with you if we avoid dropping into Germany as well?"

"Yes smart ass, it's okay with me. Looks like the enemy artillery is pounding the road and lead trucks. They are starting to "walk" the rounds down the convoy with deadly accuracy. Let's go to work."

"Lead do you see that spiral of gray smoke, drifting skyward from a hilltop through that clump of trees at four o'clock?"

"Roger that. Green flight, hold high and I'll take a look see."

"Two roger."
"Three roger."
"Four roger."

As he dove for the ground to get a closer look, Tommy spotted, hidden in that stand of trees, a Panzer Mark II tank that appeared to be directing the artillery barrage. From his altitude of 50 feet, Tommy was out of position to fire effectively.

"Green Flight, I'm going to put a rocket on the target, put your bombs on my smoke," Tommy said as he wheeled his fighter lower, using the trees as a cloaking mechanism. This maneuver behind the leafless trees was like trying to sneak the sunrise past the rooster.

'Green Two, roger."
"Green Three, roger."
"Green Four, roger."

Tommy put his rocket on target just as a hail of machine gun bullets ripped off the cowling and canopy of his shiny new aircraft. Another tank was dug in 200 yards in front of him. He fired his remaining rockets in that direction, unable to see much of anything through his oil-covered windscreen. Climbing back over the target area, he observed three other tanks filling the air with machine gun fire.

"Green Flight, there's at least five tanks down there, spread those bombs around," he said as he put his aircraft in a shallow dive and released his bombs. The air rushing through the cockpit sucked everything not tied down out into the air stream. He thought, "This is the last time I tie that scarf around my neck. It is choking the living hell out of me."

Then the bullets took out his radio and he couldn't transmit anymore. Since his headset was sucked out into the air stream it didn't matter, as wind noise and his backfiring engine made hearing any thing impossible.

Green Flight was like a bunch of kids at the county fair trying to knock the bottles over with baseballs. When the tanks' movements revealed their positions, one fighter would hurl his baseballs and knock over the bottles. Another fighter was there with his three balls in his hand ready to drop the next set of weighted containers. They were attacking and destroying with surgical accuracy. Tommy, however, was unable to maintain altitude as he made his way back to the stalled convoy. He ran out of altitude abreast of the line of trucks, and the smoking aircraft slid to a halt ten yards from the cheering troops, with its nose deep in the mud. He jumped out of the airplane, took a bow and saluted the gathering.

"Where's your convoy commander?" queried Tommy, feeling more than energized. He was ready to dance.

"He was in the lead truck, Captain. We can't tell from our position what's going on up in front of us," replied a tow-headed truck driver. This kid lied to get in the army Tommy thought. He's not a day over sixteen.

"Hey Captain, sir, I'm going up the line. Do want to ride shotgun?" an overweight buck sergeant called out from his mud-splattered jeep.

"Thanks, Sergeant," Tommy said as he jumped in. "Where was your group headed before you ran into the artillery barrage?"

"Sir, as one of the low men on the totem pole, I heard through the shit-house wall that our engineering battalion was going to Germany along with the rest of the Third Army. Some of the trucks are loaded with inflatable boats, some have floating bridge parts, and the rest have crews to put these things together in order to get our infantry across the Rhine River. There're even three platoons of infantry. Rangers I believe, that are our protective force. There wasn't supposed to be heavy resistance on this side of the river, but I guess the Krauts didn't read that part of the plan."

Pieces of five trucks, their drivers and the battalion's officer component were spilled over the Belgium country side. As the medics practiced their skills on those lucky enough to need help, a burly master sergeant was scratching his head as he looked over a blood splattered map.

Tommy walked up to him, "Sergeant, I'm Captain Thompson, the pilot of the P-47 that just got shot down. Can I be of service to your convoy commander?"

"Only if you're a chaplain and want to give him his last rites. I became the senior man when the first enemy rounds took out the commander, his staff and platoon leaders as they gathered to decide where we would try to build the floating bridge. Now that you are here may I be of service to you, sir? This map shows where we were supposed to drop off the material and men, but it appears this road and drop-off point have been zeroed in by the Germans."

Tommy looked at the map, and said "If I was running this show…"

"You are the ranking officer. This is now your show, Captain" interrupted the man. "I'm Master Sergeant McGee."

"Then Sgt. McGee, I want a platoon to follow those tank tracks and ensure that those fighters took them and their comrades out of the picture. With a positive report, send the trucks with the inflatable boats into that area. We'll hold the remainder back to set up a defensive position until we scout the enemy upstream. Any problem with that plan?…good, lets do it. Do we have a communications capability?"

"Only to the last truck with this walkie talkie. But the signal crew has been laying wire that is connected with the regiment commander unless some slew-footed Kraut hasn't tripped over it and cut it," McGee said through tobacco-stained teeth.

"Get that jeep that brought me here to take me to that truck. Contact me on your wireless when the scouting platoon reports in."

McGee waved to the driver, and the jeep bounced over next to them. Tommy got in, "Get me to the communication truck as quickly as possible," was a command he immediately regretted giving the chubby sergeant.

"Yes sir," the driver replied as the jeep lurched forward. The jeep slipped and slid, bouncing two feet in the air every time it hit a pothole. With his horn blowing a constant warning, the driver had an evil smile that a New York taxi driver would admire. Troops ducked behind their stalled trucks to keep from being a casualty or road kill.

Tommy murmured "Thanks, and wait here," as he left on wobbly legs to begin his field radio conversation with the regimental Commander. After briefing the commander on the current situation and in particular the loss of the battalion's officers, he received his orders.

"Captain it is imperative to hold that area until I can get another team of engineers and more infantry up there. Your location is one of the only two suitable for a floating bridge. You have some outstanding NCOs in that battalion, listen to them."

"Yes sir I will…and sir would you have one of your staff contact my squadron? Sir, tell them that Gray Mouse's friend needs support and will have bright yellow canvas panels pointing in the direction of the enemy on the east side of the Rhine River. The distance to the target will be 500 yards. I'm certain that even a half blind pilot will be able to see those panels."

"I'll not only make that call personally, but I'll have some one up there in four or five hours to relieve you. In the meantime captain, you are in command. Don't lose any more troops than necessary, but hold your position.

Christmas Help

It is more important than you may realize," an anxious rear echelon leader commanded."

"Yes sir," replied Tommy, now the official company commander.

The ride back was just as terrifying. A weak-kneed Tommy again said, "Thanks."

McGee stepped up to Tommy and informed him of the scouting results. "We just received word that our right flank is covered by at least one battalion of German infantry and our left flank, for all practical purposes, has only ineffective remnants of that tank cluster your fly boys busted up, sir. Any orders from battalion?" asked McGee.

"Yes, he said don't lose any more men than necessary but hold our position. I requested air support, but if granted, it will be at least two hours away. Sergeant, beef up our right flank with the infantry platoons we have available, plus any extra drivers and boat people that are sitting around picking their noses. No one moves forward, and no one gives up an inch of the high ground. We need some yellow panels laid out pointing in the direction of the enemy's main force but not closer than 500 yards. Do you have an extra weapon for me?" asked T.C.

"For Captain Thompson, we have a Thompson submachine gun. Any relationship?" McGee ventured.

"No, but I do like the sound of that name. Give me two men to carry some panels and someone to show me where our troops are dug in," requested Tommy.

At the hilltop, Tommy was pleasantly surprised at the positioning of his infantry troops that gave them a killing field 200 yards across, running down to the river, and 325 yards deep down the hill to the tree line. The spacing between the men's foxholes and trenches were too far apart, but he knew his replacements would fill in the gaps. He ran back to the road as the replacements gathered and drew weapons and ammunition. His briefing was short and concluded with…"do not give an inch. This is an important piece of real estate and it belongs to us. I want each man to carry at least one land mine and one mortar round. Make sure you have extra rounds for your rifles. After Sergeant McGee issues those items report to the Sergeant Ramerize at the top of the hill."

Having outlined what it was he wanted them to do, Tommy then led them back to their position on the firing lines. Minutes after their arrival, the experienced infantrymen had the land mines placed in crescents starting at the tree-line and staggered back every fifteen yards. A very large master sergeant, with a voice to match, called out to the replacements "I want every swinging dick to be in fox holes, ten feet apart and in line with my infantry troops. Now move out. I don't want to see anything but assholes, elbows and dirt flying."

Turning to Tommy, he said, "Captain, I have our two 30 caliber machine guns on either side of our killing field. Their field of fire interlocks this side of the mine field. Our three 81 millimeter mortars have their rounds set to air burst six to ten feet above the ground on the other side of the tree line. They will commence firing in an overlapping search and traverse pattern when the first land mines explodes. They will continue their routine until I tell them to stop. If your replacement troops will aim and fire their weapons I believe we can hold the high ground and that is one big if."

"Sergeant Ramerize, you have obviously done this before. Anything you want me to do?"

"Yes sir, stay out of the line of fire and keep those new troops firing their weapons. They are not infantry so they need to be motivated to look out at the enemy and fire at them. If they hit them that will be a pleasant surprise."

Tommy climbed into the turret of one of the damaged panzers, located to the rear of the firing line. He looked over his battle arena. He shouted down to Sergeant Ramerize, "We can defend this place." He moved about in the turret and noticed the machine gun turned easily on its grooved sliding race and did not appear to be damaged He was able to achieve a good sight picture down the middle of the crescent. He started to get out of the tank when a large enemy force broke out of the tree line and ran into the freshly placed mines. This surprise stopped the advance, but only for a moment. The next surge put them in the next crescent of mines and then the battle was joined. The infantry men had good control over the new replacements. "Hold your fire, men," Ramerize roared, and the men nervously held their fire. The

German troops advanced to within 100 yards and the Ramerize's command "Commence firing," let loose a thundering salvo of bullets. The popping of the mortar rounds as they left the tubes were right on cue. The screaming of the enemy infantrymen as the shrapnel tore into their bodies brought a tight lip grin to the face of Master Sergeant Ramerize. His machine gunners wasted no time in neutralizing any foot soldier that made it through the mine field.

Tommy tried the tank's machine gun and when it discharged the first rounds, he was unexpectedly shocked that the damn thing worked. The errant rounds took a few branches off some trees, scared a couple birds into flying and amazed the troops on both sides of the battle. Taking aim, he was able to hit an enemy mortar team before they got a round off. A machine gun crew was also dispatched along with three men who tried to replace them. The motley friendly replacement troops, having gotten over their initial fear and seeing that their foes could bleed just like they could, became darn right vicious. They fired their weapons, reloaded, fired again and kept repeating, all the time yelling and screaming like a Chicago street gang.

From his vantage point, Tommy could see the enemies muzzle flashes that looked like fireflies in the tree line. He fired a three second burst in that direction. This worked rather well until some mathematical genius from the University of Berlin figured out where the deadly pearls of death were coming from. He was now the designated target of opportunity for some very pissed off German troops. Fortunately most of the bullets bounced off the panzer's tough sides. The rest sailed over Tommy's head with the sound of angry hornets. He silenced a couple more positions, then ran out of ammunition. He slid, then fell off the back of the tank, spraying the enemy area with his submachine gun as he dove for the nearest trench. Joining two replacement troops, he said, "Nice work, men…keep up the good shooting and don't close your eyes when you pull the trigger."

One young truck driver blushed like he got caught with his hand in the cookie jar by his momma. "Captain, I really did have them open most of the time. I'll do better."

Tommy was taken aback that his smart-ass comment put the young man on the edge of shame. "Trooper, let's trade weapons. Short bursts and only at a target." The young man's eyes were opened as wide as Orphan Annie's. His smile became a sneer that would make Edward G. Robinson envious. I believe I have just created a warrior, thought Tommy as he test fired the M-1 Rifle.

"Cover me as I check on the troops," he yelled as he made for the next foxhole.

Right beside him the kid with the sub machine gun. "I meant stay in the trench and cover me." He grabbed him and put him in a hole with one of the rangers. He continued his rounds encouraging his troops to keep firing.

He was surprised that the kid kept following him like a puppy dog.

"All right, give me some covering fire," he yelled.

"What's that mean?"

"It means shoot at the enemy so they won't shoot at us," Tommy replied, shaking his head.

"Oh."

Miraculously, all his men were alive, some scared. His nose told him that a couple had crapped in their pants, but the scattered expended shell casings indicated they were firing their weapons. "Men, you are doing better than good…keep pouring the lead at them," he yelled to them as he scurried to the next foxhole, and so far no wounded…unbelievable! There was sporadic firing as he crawled his way back to the top of the hill, almost all of it from his men as they gave him covering fire. He was back in the trench as the first fighter aircraft came in and bombed the enemy positions. He counted sixteen P-47s whose pilots put on an air show that lasted nearly an hour.

Sgt. Ramerize hurried over to Tommy. "Sir, I don't know what in the hell you told those replacements, but after three years fighting the Nazis, I have never seen such intense firing from new troops. If they don't want to drive trucks any more, I'll take them, each and every one of those swinging dicks."

"Sergeant Ramerize, send out a squad to reconnoiter the area in an effort to prepare for the next wave of attacks."

Before the squad could return, a Lt. Col. Henry crawled his way to his trench and with bated breath said, "Captain, I'm your replacement. How many men did you lose?"

"None, sir. And our recon people will be back in short order… I'm sure with an estimate of the enemy's strength and position," answered T.C..

"None. Who the hell set this up, and where did all these infantry men come from, and what's that kid doing with that submachine gun?"

"Sir, I relied on sergeant Ramerize's infantry men to set up the killing field, lay the mines and position the replacements. Master Sergeant McGee gathered the drivers and boat crewmen as replacements to fill in the gaps in the firing line, and that young man, PFC Jacobs, to whom I gave that submachine gun, is my body guard," a calm Captain Thompson replied, almost out of breath.

"You were his body guard?" he asked the baby faced private.

"Yes, sir, except for when he was shooting the shit out the Nazis from that tank," answered PFC Levy Jacobs, standing much taller than his five foot five inch body. "Sir, I've been in Europe six months and being a body guard is a hell of a lot more fun than driving them trucks."

Turning to Tommy Lieutenant Colonel Henry said, "Captain, you had outstanding results. Through some minor miracle, you and this motley crew held this strategic piece of real estate. Now I'm going to get that damn bridge built. After your squad reports in with the battle assessment, there's a jeep going back to headquarters. They will find a way to get you to your squadron. Jacobs, you're now my body guard. Put an extra stripe on that sleeve. Fun… sweet Jesus he calls this madness fun."

Chapter 25

Tommy massaged his really sore butt from the two day, 250-mile ride back to his base in everything from jeeps to four by four trucks. He thanked the last driver as he headed towards the operation officer's tent still trying to rub the pain out from his buttocks.

"Well, I'll be damned," a smiling Amos Jackson declared as he field stripped his Camel cigarette outside the operation officer's hut. "Underneath that mud and grime, I believe there's a German ace. You've now been shot down a total of five times, and I don't know if the Army Air Corp can afford to have you flying their airplanes, but keep up the good work. The squadron voted and you won the 'Better Him Than Me' award. I think you better spruce up before you go in there. There's not much sympathy flowing towards you since you gave the ops officer that cock and bull story about your time with De Gaulle."

Tommy reached in his pocket and with two fingers

dangled the Croix de Guerre in Amos's face and said, "Should I send it back?"

"Double damn, is this going to be fun. Allow me to escort you in…the cleaning chore can wait."

"Damn it, Thompson," began Major Peck, "the wing commander sends you off to get a high-level ass-chewing and you end up with another medal. I send you off to deliver eight brand-new Jugs to us and only seven make it here. On top of that, your award elements arrived this morning from the French, along with a dispatch from a Lt. Col. Wade Henry recommending an award for your leadership and bravery under fire defeating a numerically superior ground force. Are you for real or just an award and decorations officer's wet dream? Now get the hell out of here and clean up! You are stinking up my office. Turn in your flying gear, Captain. Congratulations, you're going home."

"Is the war over?" a flabbergasted Tommy asked.

"No, just yours here in Europe. I don't have anymore details except six of my most experienced officers are on that list. Go get washed up, get some rest, and we'll talk when I get more information."

"Yes sir." he left the room, feeling that a large load had been removed from his shoulders.

"Hey Tommy, I'm one of the others going home with you. I'm guessing that we are on the way to the Pacific theatre of operations. We might be able to get a couple, two, maybe three Zeros and make ace," ventured Amos.

"Deep down inside, I don't think that's going to happen. I'm betting that we're going to end the war training snotty-nosed aviation cadets to be pilots. I would rather take my chances in combat than sit in the back seat of a PT-19," lamented Tommy. "With an inexperienced student at the controls of the "Cradle of Heroes" I know damn well my toes will involuntarily pull my socks down into my boots. Well, we are stuck with whatever the assignment is, but it's our ticket home. Let's check with admin and see what they have for us."

"What did I tell you, Amos? Our group's mode of transportation to the states is an ocean liner out of Antwerp. Whoever needs us, and no one seems to know who that is, doesn't have enough clout to get us on an airliner or military air."

Chapter 26

The commercial ship vibrated violently as the engines' power was increased to pull away from the dock at Antwerp. Flying the American flag, this leased ship from the Netherlands was on its twentieth voyage through the remnants of the German submarine fleet. The ship's captain paced back and forth across the bridge.

"Is there something we should be concerned with Captain?" His executive officer quietly asked."

"I will not relax until we rendezvous with the destroyer escort. We have nine hundred officers and war weary men crammed on board this vessel. It was built to carry five hundred people in luxurious comfort. The ships complement brings the total to eleven hundred and fifty souls. That's my concern and I hope it's yours too.

"Yes sir, it is…I pray every night for a safe crossing."

On deck watching the fog roll over the ship, Tommy and Amos watched in silence as the shoreline disappeared in the swirling sea fog. "I hope this murk stays with us all the way home," Tommy said, breaking the silence.

"I was hoping to acquire a nice suntan so my lily white body won't scare all those warm legged Texas girls I'm hoping to romance."

"You're going to need more than a suntan to land one of those sweetie pies."

"Let's check out our lavish quarters. Maybe we can just sleep our way across the Atlantic."

Inside their ten foot by ten foot cabin, Tommy asked Amos, "Upper or lower?"

"Since I don't know how steady your stomach is going to be when we get out of this river and onto the rolling sea, I'll take the upper."

"Amos you put one drop of puke on me and our friendship is over," warned Tommy. Their duffle bags and two boxes marked Top Secret had been put up against the bulkhead. The boxes contained whiskey and playing cards.

The cruise back to the states started off well enough. The first day the sea was calm. The food was better than average and was served hot to the officer component. The booze was almost nonexistent except for those, like Tommy and Amos, who hand carried theirs on board in boxes marked Top Secret.

Two days out to sea a klaxon sounded a practice abandon ship drill. This task was exercised even as the sea's swells had the ship's bow out of the water momentarily.

When it slammed back into the angry waters, the entire ship groaned. For those unfortunate few that were in the brig, located two decks directly aft of the bow, the prisoners considered this cruel and unusual punishment.

"Holy cow Amos, where did all these men come from? Their faces match their olive drab fatigues. More than a few of them look pretty green around the gills. After the drill let's see what kind of accommodations the troops have. We'll follow the last ones below deck," Tommy yelled as he hung on to the ship's rail as the ship rolled starboard ten degrees.

Down they went, slipping and sliding on the slick metal stairs. "Looks like they welded the bunks eight high along the ship's six hundred foot length, stopping only for the bulkheads that define the compartments. I'm guessing that there's eighteen inches between the rows and it looks like four rows across the beam of the ship. There is maybe one small table for each compartment," exclaimed Amos. "Let's check out their mess."

There were men already lined up for breakfast... their appointed shift interrupted by the abandon ship drill. "Do you see those serving trays sliding down that metal table? It appears to be a game of chance to end up with the tray you started with. That sea water coming in through that broken porthole can't make the green eggs and the shit on the shingle taste much like they are suppose to taste," commented Tommy. As one man went to sit at a table another threw up next to him which caused the first man to lose whatever he had in his stomach. "Let move on," Amos said tugging at Tommy's sleeve, his face starting to lose its color as the odor from the grease and puke penetrated the stale air.

As they wandered through the lower deck, Amos grabbed Tommy's arm and said, "Partner, my nose tells me we are headed towards an open latrine. My adventurous spirit has just been gassed and died. I'm going topside."

Angry four letter words mixed with laughter came from the latrine that Tommy couldn't resist looking into. There were at least twenty men sitting on a long gray metal bench answering nature's call. Their butts hung over a channel of continuous rushing flush water.

What brought on the angry outburst and laughter? Someone had balled up a wad of toilet paper, set it on fire and launched it down the canal. Those with burned butts or worse were ready to start world war three. All others were laughing so hard it was impossible to determine the culprit or to finish what they started.

As a staff sergeant pointed him to the stairs, Tommy asked, "Are the men going to be able to survive this trip?"

"Captain, if this ship was a Spanish galleon and we had to paddle it to America, we would. We will make it because we're going home and away from the war."

That evening in the officer's mess, steaks were being served by enlisted men who volunteered for kitchen duty because they wanted a break from the misery below deck. Tommy went back for seconds and sat there playing with his food until all the other officers left the area. "Hey Sarge," he called out, "would you take care of this for me? Seems my eyes are bigger than my stomach."

"Not to worry sir, it won't go to waste."

The ship rolled port and starboard fifteen to twenty degrees for the next five days. A pleasant surprise occurred when Tommy and Amos found their sea legs and were able to explore every deck and even the engine room. The noise in the boiler room was almost deafening.

"Where's all that steam coming from?" yelled Tommy pointing at a building cloud forward of the boiler.

"Stay low and I'll show you," a sweaty chief petty officer roared, picking up a straw broom. Holding the broom upright above his head he moved in a duck like fashion across room. Ten feet from the cloud of vapor the straw bristles fell from the broom as if cut by an invisible razor.

"What happened?" a red faced Tommy blurted.

"A pinhole leak in a pipe with six hundred pounds of pressure per square inch is what's happening. Stay low and moved back to the stairs. We'll take care of this. Thanks for visiting …we don't get much company down here."

Top side Amos queried to nobody in particular, "Are those guys fishing for sharks with those ropes?"

A deck hand answered, "No sir. This is the Captain's way to keep the enlisted men busy and the decks clean with mops and sea water. When the mops needed to be cleansed of the puke and food, the mop heads are tied to a rope and thrown over board. After ten minutes the mops are pulled in…clean and white as snow. It's an endless chore that keeps the enlisted men from getting cabin fever and out of fights."

The card games were endless. "Let's try our luck, Amos."

"As many times as you've been shot down, I'm betting you haven't much luck left."

I'll cover that wager, Bartholomew said, reaching for a parcel of luck.

Acey Deucy was by far the most popular pastime because the hands were dealt fast and winning was pure luck. A player would bet that the third card dealt to him would rank between his two hole cards.

Even on the last days of the trip when the ship's bow went up and slammed into the waves continuously, the games continued. "What was the max bet?" Tommy shouted over the noise from the ship's engine screws that sounded like a banshee gargling when they came up out of the water. Holding on to his hole cards as the ship shook like a hound trying to shed water from its coat, he answered his own question. "Never mind I'll cover the pot."

Tommy was forced to quit this game after two days of winning. He took seriously a fellow officer's threat to throw him over board. His slightly irate comrade leaned across the table and remarked, "Only someone blessed with a card shark guardian angel could consistently win at this game."

I have to do some thing with this luck...besides, I wasn't very good at card games and it regularly cost me my pay check at the aerodrome officers' chalet, Bartholomew recalled.

Tommy switched to poker and lost half the money back to his friends. This token loss to his friends didn't do much to smooth out the ruffled feathers, but when Tommy put two forty ounce bottles of Wild Turkey on the table, all was forgiven.

After ten days of evading the German submarine force on the Atlantic crossing, docking at the port in New York seemed anti-climatic. Tommy and his group were pulled aside prior to stepping on to the gangplank to disembark.

"Gentlemen, the Captain wishes to speak to all of you. Please follow me," came an order, not an invitation, from the Captain's aide.

"Damn," murmured Amos not quite discreetly," I knew putting top secret on those cases would get us in trouble."

"If you knew that, why did you pack an extra case?" whispered Tommy nudging Amos in the ribs with his elbow.

After a few pleasantries were exchanged and a cup of coffee offered and accepted, the Captain announced, "Gentlemen your new assignment has been cancelled.

You may proceed to your home address and await further orders. I see by the decorations adorning your tunics that you all have earned a well deserved rest. Thompson, I don't know what your role in this conflict has been, but the next time you're on board my ship you are invited to my table and we shall trade sea stories for air stories."

"When you are together again sir, ask him how he got to be a German ace," interjected a smiling Amos.

A puzzled ship's captain looked Tommy in the eye and said "Really?"

Blushing, Tommy nodded and in his own defense countered "I was never shot down by an airplane, only by enemy ground fire."

"My, my, you must have one hell of a tired guardian angel," the Captain said dismissing the group. Bartholomew agreed whole heartedly with the captain.

"This is a great way to start the month of May," an elated Amos remarked as they stepped on American soil. "Where you headed, Tommy?"

"Back to my beautiful wife in northern Wisconsin. How about you?"

"Where else but deep in the heart of west Texas," drawled Amos. "On to the phone booths. Any one got a nickel?"

Chapter 27

"What do you mean you're in New York? When did you get there? When are you leaving? Have you called Peggy? Or your Father?" screamed a joyful Mary Hanover.

"I am on leave between assignments, and I got here today and don't know how long I'll be on leave. I don't know Peggy's phone number and haven't called my dad. There are at least a hundred GI's waiting for this phone. Please tell Peggy and my dad that I'll call when I get away from the port. I don't know how I can arrange transportation, but I'll be starting to your house immediately. Tell Peggy I love her. I hope you are all well, goodbye," a tearful T.C. hurriedly mumbled.

Tommy and Amos caught a base bus to the army air terminal where a C-47 pilot in the coffee shop spotted them looking forlorn and a little confused. After trading a war story or two, he offered, "I'm going to Chicago… want to ride along?"

"Want to? Hell, we'll even pay you," replied Amos.

"Buddy, I don't accept cash but you two can buy me a drink or two at Chicago as that's my layover stop." This proposition Amos and Tommy tripped over each other to accept.

At the Chicago airport bar, the C-47 pilot introduced them to a group of airman ferrying B-25's to the west coast. Amos hooked up with a fellow Texan who bragged, "If your farm has a half decent cow pasture and not too many oil wells to run into, I'll have you milking cows tomorrow morning."

One first lieutenant, short in stature but long on cockiness, invited Tommy along, warning him, "I'm going to be practicing low-altitude night navigation and it might be uncomfortable…even a little bit scary. But I promise you I'm not suicidal."

Strapping in the co-pilot's seat, Tommy remarked, "I bet you five dollars that you can't make Truax Field, Wisconsin with only one heading change and one change of altitude from 100 feet to 500 feet for 30 seconds to check a navigation point."

"You're on," an arrogant and confident pilot-in-command replied as he looked over his map to see where in the hell Truax Field was located. Eyeballing a heading towards Madison, Wisconsin, then writing down some communication and navigation frequencies, he taxied the aircraft out to the runway. Shortly after takeoff, the lieutenant dimmed the instrument lights in an effort to better his night vision. "Not a whole hell of a lot to see out there, is there?" Tommy asked as he leaned forward in an effort to see better.

"That sliver of a moon helps when it reflects off all those lakes. And it really helps when it shines up those railroad tracks."

"Do you see that red light in our twelve o'clock position?"

"Must be the radio station I have tuned on the low frequency direction finder. That's our midway point. I'll pull up in the next 30 seconds or so and the needle should swing to our tail."

"And if it doesn't?"

"Then I owe you five bucks."

The needle swung pointing to the tail. "I don't think I'll need to pull up to check my navigation…want to double the bet?"

"Not unless you really screw up and run us into those thunderstorms that are lighting up the sky over in our two o'clock position.

"Hell those are at least one hundred miles away. We'll be on the ground and those storms will still be grinding away fifty miles north."

On the ramp at Truax, Tommy handed the lieutenant five dollars saying, "Don't let this go to your head, but you're good. I wish you well, the best of luck and thanks again for one hell of an exciting flight."

Bartholomew sighed with relief when the flight was over, reminding himself of a mental note he made one stormy night over France…*"That night flying was meant for owls."*

"Mary, I'm at Truax Field. What's Peggy's phone number?"

"Tommy, I'll call her and have her meet you at the front gate. It's almost nine o'clock and it'll take her about a half hour to get there. She's driving your 1939 Buick convertible that your dad had put back in excellent shape…he even found a set of wide white wall tires to put on it. We're so excited. She's so excited. Your dad said that he has made hotel reservations for you two at the Concourse Hotel in Madison. He didn't know when you would get there, so he made it for the next three days. He said the company would take care of the bill. Call me when you start this way…in the next day or two," a devilish Mary purred.

"Mary, I've given your telephone number to my army personnel officer as a good number to reach me at when he has orders for me. Please don't tell the officer 'to kiss off,' as my British friends are keen on saying."

"Tommy, you know I wouldn't be anything but nice to a man in uniform", she promised but she had her fingers crossed.

Tommy made small talk with the guard at the front gate. He turned from looking down the road to looking at his watch when this familiar voice called out to him, "Hey fly boy, you looking for a good time?"

He didn't bother to open the door of the convertible. He made a very respectable standing high jump from the curb into the front seat and had his beautiful wife in the most tender embrace a horny fighter pilot could muster.

"Captain, if you're going to park there, you might consider putting the top up," a wide eyed military policeman suggested.

Coming up for breath, a smiling Tommy replied, "Right you are, Sergeant." He took over the driver's seat and the Buick made a screeching U-turn and was almost at the base boundary when a red flashing light forced him to the side of the road.

"Okay cowboy what's the rush? Your driver's license please."

Tommy interrupted the Dane County sheriff, "Officer, I've been back in the states less than one day, and this is my wife who I haven't seen in one year, and we are on are way to the Concourse hotel…"

Looking at a couple rows of service ribbons and an adoring wife, the officer ordered Tommy, "Follow me." Sirens and flashing lights led Tommy and Peggy to a parking place in front of the hotel.

"Welcome home, Captain," the law enforcement officer said as he opened the Buick's door. His hand salute identified him as a former military man. Tommy came to attention as he returned this greeting. A very much appreciative Mrs. Thompson kissed the officer on his cheek and then was led into the hotel by the man for whom she longed to hold.

* * *

Tommy was able to wrangle an extra day's stay at the

hotel and he was able to escort Peggy around the campus to visit with her professors.

"Your wife's course work is in the top one percent of her classes," the stern face department head announced. "I've consulted with her professors and they see no reason for her to take the final exams scheduled next week. Peggy's been burning the candle at both ends to stay at the head of her classmates. Captain, see to it that she gets some rest…she looks a bit exhausted."

"I promise to go right to bed as soon as we finished the tour of the campus," Peggy quickly answered. Then her face blushed bright red as a smile spread across the department head's face. "You know what I mean," she stammered.

"Mrs. Thompson, I may be old but I still remember my homecoming after the last war. Go…enjoy each other."

Peggy was sitting on the bed with a large hotel towel wrapped around her wet body. She had waited until the last minute to telephone her mom with their travel plans. "Mom, we'll be leaving Madison in about an hour and should be home around two o'clock. Tommy hopes you would have some cinnamon rolls when we get there," a giggling Peggy informed her. With great reluctance, she tried to push Tommy's hand from her wet breast.

"I think I can manage that. Drive safe," responded Mary, hanging up her phone.

As Peggy's phone hit the cradle, she rolled over Tommy, pinning him to the bed. She swung her nipples across his face, whispering, "You can be most annoying and I must teach you to behave." She eased her wet body down gently onto Tommy, who was now on his best behavior.

Two hours later they headed north to Peggy's home in Prairie View. The sun was shinning brightly and glistened off Peggy's hair, giving it a multi color, deep reddish brown sheen as it flowed in the air. The convertible's black canvas top was down as Tommy and Peggy enjoyed the warm spring air. Rolling Wisconsin countryside was lush with cornfields that stretched from one hill to the next flashed by. As the thick stands of pine trees took over the landscape, the cool air's slight movement encouraged Peggy to nestle closer to her love. She moved her hand in a not so casual manner to Tommy's inner thigh. At the first wayside park, the convertible's top came up. Another hour was added to their journey.

The sign on the Hanover's store's door read "Tommy and Peggy, we're at the Moose Hall."

The crowd inside cheered to greet them as the surprised couple stepped inside. They were swept first into the arms of the Hanovers, then to the embrace of the senior Thompson. Father Hurley and Joe Marsh pretty much did a group hug and then someone started singing "God Bless America." As the last strain of "...home sweet home" echoed through the hall, Father Hurley gave a quick blessing over the enormous brunch that Tommy's dad had arranged with Mary and John's help. No one was excluded from the invitations, and many well wishers left their fields unattended in order to greet Tommy and his wife. Everyone welcomed their hometown hero. But he wasn't a wartime hero to Peggy. She was just happy to have the love of her life home. The brunch included an orange juice and champagne concoction that was supposed to be a harmless beverage to satisfy one's thirst. The only unfortunate outcome of the party was more than a few of the older farmers and their wives thought it was the best damn orange juice they had ever tasted and couldn't get enough of it. This resulted in the fields being neglected until noon the next day.

The large group splintered into tables of eight to ten and the common thread of conversation was the news of Hitler's death that the radio had announced several days ago. Tommy and Peggy were in the two percent that missed this announcement because they concentrated their every effort to closing out the world as they rediscovered each other. Along with everyone else they were thrilled that the war in Europe would soon be over.

Two days later, May eighth, 1945, the German Chancellor surrendered unconditionally to the Allied powers. A special mass of Thanksgiving was given that Tuesday afternoon at Saint Teresa's church where the Hanover family and the Thompson family were amongst the crowded congregation. It was a solemn, long and quiet affair, Tommy's grim face reflected the sacrifices that America, and in particular the sons and daughters of America, had made. His grim look gave way to a smile

Christmas Help

when the four year old boy in front of him, twirling his rosary on his finger, said in a not so quiet voice, "Hang on Jesus we're almost done."

Chapter 28

"Bartholomew, what are you doing here? You are not finished!" An uninhabited island in the Aleutian chain disappeared under a forty foot high wave as God spoke.

"But God, the war in Europe is over. Thompson is in the arms of his sweetheart and I love the way you redecorated your chamber. The reflection pool needs a brilliant light shining into it, maybe if you created a nova..."

"The conflicts are not over, Bartholomew!" Lake Erie's waters tossed fishing boats into shallows of the Cuyahoga River.

"But..."

"I have given all my children choices. Your choice is Thompson or the tumbleweeds. And by the by Bartholomew that "luck" I prescribed for you to spread around is not for gambling."

There was a moment of peace in heaven and on earth as Bartholomew departed thinking, "An angel's work is never done...and did God say conflict or conflicts?"

Sitting on the edge of the river bank, their fishing lines' cork bobbers floating neglected in the mid morning sun, Tommy kissed Peggy's hand. "Careful where you put your lips," Peggy cautioned. "I just put a night crawler on my hook."

Tommy looked into her gray eyes then stuck her fingers in his mouth and mumbled, "Tastes like baloney to me." Backing away a few inches, he put a serious look on his face. "I'm surprised I haven't heard from the army about my next assignment. It's not that this last month hasn't been like heaven on earth…it has. But I have this feeling that your mother has been playing cat and mouse with me."

"Why do you think that?" Peggy asked, trying her best to hide the sly grin creeping across her face.

"Every time I ask her if the army called, she puts her hands behind her back and says 'No.'"

Peggy laughed and confessed, "She does that so that you won't be able to see that she's crossed her fingers."

"Damn it," an irritated Tommy said as he started to roll in his line.

"Where you off to in such a huff?"

"I'm going back to the store. I need to telephone the army personnel officer."

"Let's not waste this beautiful day. I packed a picnic basket, along with a bottle of my dad's homemade wine and for desert, a nice soft blanket," a mischievous Peggy proposed.

"Hey! Your bobber just disappeared," yelled Tommy.

"The hell with the bobber," Peggy almost sang as she reached for the blanket and Tommy.

"Catch anything?" inquired Peggy's dad as he interrupted a war story with Tommy's father.

"Well the bobber went down once but we were too slow in reeling it in and it got away," Tommy explained.

"At least you had a little action, so the day wasn't a total waste."

Blushing, Peggy excused herself and Tommy made the telephone call to the army personnel office at Truax Field. Glaring his disapproval at his mother-in-law, whose smug smile indicated she really wasn't sorry for her little white lies that kept the army officials at bay. After many transfers of his telephone call, an irate Major yelled, "Thompson I've called you three times this week and some lady keeps telling me to 'kiss off.' I hope that wasn't your wife."

"No sir, I believe that's my mother-in-law, who thinks I've done enough to save the world from the Axis menace," Tommy replied with little conviction. "Do you have an assignment for me, sir?"

"As a matter of fact I do. I believe you'll enjoy flying with a special mission fighter squadron out of Eglin Field, Florida. I can't tell you much more over the telephone due to the classified nature of the mission. You'll report to the squadron on July 2nd and you'll be there for three months in a temporary duty status. I don't have a follow on assignment for you because the war with Japan is in a state of flux. I'll have your paperwork sent out to you. It should be there in three days. If you want to drive your car, I'll authorize that mode of transportation and include some gas stamps in the package. Any questions?"

"Sir, I'd like to drive and is there any possibility that my wife may accompany me?" asked Tommy.

"Captain, you may bring your wife, but at your expense. There's no base housing available for married officers in a temporary duty status and the civilian real estate market is oversaturated with military families. Rumor has it that chicken coops are being rented out with a high premium. If you don't have any more questions I wish you luck and good day."

"Good day, sir," a deflated Tommy replied.

"Well is it good news or bad news," came the cry from the family gathered at the kitchen table.

"It's bittersweet in that I'll be flying fighters, and Peggy can come with me, but the housing picture is horrible. I'll not bring her if she has to stay in a dilapidated shack," announced Tommy.

"Another separation?" cried Peggy. "Well I'm coming with you even if we have to live in a tent."

"Don't make a decision right now you two. Maybe something will turn up," his father said as he turned to leave. "Mary and John, thanks for the hospitality and you kids have some fun. It's going to be a beautiful summer.

I'll be out of state for most of the month pursuing a large government contract. Wish me luck as the company can certainly use the business."

Two weeks later as Tommy and Peggy returned from a blueberry picking outing, Tommy said, "There's Dad's car. Seems he can't get enough of your dad's wine and your mother's cinnamon rolls. I prefer coffee with my rolls but my dad likes the bottle maybe a little too much. Hope he got the contract he wanted."

"Don't judge old people darling, because one day we will be in that white hair group," teased Peggy.

Mary saw that bucket full of blueberries. Her sarcasm was hard not to miss. "You two finally went into the woods and brought something edible back. Your lack of success gathering strawberries, mushrooms, raspberries or fish can be attributed to the blanket that you forgot today. Sit down, the coffee is hot and so are the cinnamon rolls."

After the chuckles died down, Tommy father announced, "I have some very good news. I got the contract. Which means a sizable expansion for the company. And as luck would have it, part of that expansion will be in Florida. With that in mind, I bought some property with a house on the beach in Destin, Florida. That's a little town not too far from Eglin Field. A friend of mine, a former leatherneck, and now a big time real estate broker, had this property and said it would meet my present and future needs. The house is furnished and maybe a little large for your stay in Florida, but I will rent it to you for twenty five dollars a month plus utilities. Water comes from a well so all you'll have to pay is for the telephone. The electricity bill will be picked up by the owner of the property, Thompson Industries. There's only one condition that might be a problem."

"What's the catch, Dad?"

"There's a guest house on the property that Peggy's parents might want to stay in from time to time if it's alright with you...hell, they'll stay there even if its not alright with you. Deal?"

Peggy squealed with delight as she ran over and hugged Tommy's dad's neck, almost knocking him off his chair.

"I guess that means you accept," a red face father in law said.

* * *

The gold star flag hanging in the window was the only testimony to the reason for the sale of the beach property in Destin, Florida. After the only child of the McAlister's was shot down and killed in a B-17 raid over Germany, the couple sank into deep depression. Three months after their son died, the couple headed their small boat into the raging waters of the gulf one cold January night. Their wrecked, empty boat washed up near Panama City five days later.

Christmas Help

The screened-in porch that encircled the first floor shaded Tommy as he carried Peggy over the threshold of their first home. They both felt the warmth that wasn't from the midday sun but from decades of love the former home owner's family had for one another.

"Tommy, this house is beautiful and so well kept that I'm afraid that I'll be spending all my time trying to keep the sand off the floor."

"I forgot to tell you that when Dad, or more correctly the company, purchased the property, the housekeeper and gardener were available. So somewhere in this cute, six bedroom beach house, there are accommodations for this married caretaker couple."

"You forgot! I'm going to do something drastic to improve your memory. Let's find the bedroom."

"Excuse me, Captain," a strong male voice interrupted. "I'm Jeremiah and this is my wife Sarah. Sarah will be happy to show you the house and I'll take your bags to the master bedroom."

Startled by unexpected appearance of this handsome, older black couple, Tommy extended his hand and offered, "I'm Tommy Thompson and this is my wife Peggy. We didn't realize you were here."

"Captain, I'm sorry we surprised you, but when we heard voices, we came to investigate. The real estate man told us to expect you, but he didn't know when you would arrive. We hope the house is in acceptable condition. Sarah, take the Captain and his wife and show them the house. Afterward, if the Captain agrees, I'll serve some lemonade and cakes on the porch facing the water."

"Jeremiah, this house would pass the inspection of the most nitpicking drill sergeant in the army. Your offer of refreshments is most agreeable and delightful. I'll unload the car…"

"That won't be necessary, Captain. I'll do that. Please go with your wife and Sarah," interrupted Jeremiah.

After the tour, sipping the sweet lemonade, Peggy remarked, "Tommy, I never imagined sand being this white and water being this blue. Let's go walk on the beach and see if the water is warm enough to swim in."

"We can do that tomorrow, honey. I want to drive to the base to find out how long it takes to get there and to locate the squadron's orderly room. I want to sign in bright and early Monday morning," responded Tommy. Looking over his shoulder, he asked Jeremiah, "Is there a short cut out to the base?"

"Yes sir. I have prepared a map for you that will take a half hour off your trip. I've also included the house's telephone number and the street address. Will you and your lady be having dinner here? Sarah's a fine cook, especially with seafood."

"If you have no objection Peggy, does a seven o'clock dinner meet with your approval?" asked Tommy.

"Yes it does. I'm looking forward to my first taste of fresh seafood," answered Peggy. "Sarah, will you allow me to watch? I'm a new bride and cooking hasn't been a chore I've had to learn, except for cinnamon rolls… that's Tommy's favorite."

"Miz. Thompson, cooking isn't a chore if you do it for a loved one. Perhaps you can teach me how you Yankees make cinnamon rolls."

A flight of four P-51's flew low over Tommy's car as he crossed the bridge linking the peninsula with the mainland. They were in echelon and pitched up into a downwind leg and then to a descending base leg. It appeared to Tommy that they were using his car as a target on their simulated attacks. From a pilot's point of view, the attack lacked the altitude needed to complete the maneuver. This unfortunate prediction for the number four aircraft proved to be a correct assumption.

The aircraft was pulling streamers of condense moist air as the aircraft pancaked into the water with an ear piercing slap. It slid to a stop almost under the bridge. Tommy stopped the car and waited for the pilot to jettison the canopy. He could see the pilot slumped forward but was motionless. He saw a trickle of blood ooze from his mouth and ears. Tommy jumped over the wooden rail and fell fifteen feet into the water. As Tommy's head popped to the surface, he thought, the water's warmer than I expected. The aircraft was sinking slowly and he struggled to pull the emergency lanyard that opened the canopy. The canopy popped open, but the pilot still wasn't moving. After he released he pilot's seat belt and shoulder harness, it took every bit of muscle Tommy had to pull the pilot clear of the aircraft before it sank.

Tommy struggled to unfasten the parachute straps. He managed to inflate the pilot's may west that carried them up to salty water's surface. They bobbed up and down as the swells of the brine rolled over their faces. Keeping their heads above water was a losing proposition as he tried to swim to the shore. His arms struggled to move them forward. He felt his luck was running out when someone shouted, "Grab the life preserver… it's to your right." Tommy reached out and hung on to the round life preserver and the pilot as two men pulled them on to deck of a motor boat.

"The pilot's dead," offered a distinguished looking man.

"Are you sure?" questioned Tommy.

"With twenty five years of practicing medicine under my belt, I'm sure." What's your name son?"

"Tommy Thompson, sir. And yours?"

"Dr. Dan Bowers. My friend Billy and I saw the plane crash and watched you jump off the bridge. We were impressed that you'd take that kind of risk for a stranger."

"Someone pulled me out of the water when my plane crashed a couple years ago, and I was hoping to return the favor. Doctor, can you take care of the body? I mean get it to the air base. I'm new to this area and haven't the foggiest idea on where to go."

"Yes, we can do that," assured the doctor. "And what do we do with you?"

"Drop me off close to the bridge and I'll take my car back to the home we are renting."

"There's only one house on the other end of that bridge and so you must be renting the McAlister's home. You have to be a big butter and egg man in order to afford that place," teased Dr. Dan.

"No sir, I'm just a poor fighter pilot with a father who has deep pockets," Tommy yelled as he jumped back into the water.

"Watch for snakes as you climb that bank. Good luck," a concerned man of medicine called out.

Bartholomew was already busy pacifying a nest of rattlers that Tommy had disturbed. He had to move fast to put his wing next to Tommy's leg as another tried to sink his fangs in his soggy pants. *If I was human, that bite would have finished me off. In my present state, it tickles.*

Tommy was met at the rear of the house by Jeremiah, who was pulling weeds in that part of the garden where the okra was growing. "Captain, you should really use a bathing suit if you're going to be swimming. That salt water is hard on those silver tan uniforms. If you would take them off, I'll try soaking them in fresh water to see if I can save them. There's a towel inside the back door. I think the ladies will be surprised to see you home early and half naked," an amused Jeremiah chuckled.

"Well that was a quick trip," Peggy said, glancing up from a bowl of dough she was kneading. "What happened? Did you wreck the car? Are you hurt? There has to be a story you can share, but first towel off a little before you drip water across the floor." Sarah didn't look up from shucking oysters but had a hint of a smile on her face because the new bride was able to talk straight to her man without embarrassing him.

"There was a plane crash up by the bridge. I jumped in the water and pulled the pilot out of the plane. A Doctor Dan Bowers and his friend pulled us both into his boat. I'm not hurt, just wet."

"Now that's a story. A real thriller. Wow. Is the pilot okay?"

"No, honey. Hate to say it, but he's dead. It was the end of a stupid maneuver that shouldn't have been started. It appeared the flight leader had his head up and locked. Come here honey. Let me wipe those tears. Jeremiah, forget those clothes and hold Sarah."

He held Peggy's hands, whispering in a soft voice, "Flying's not forgiving of bad judgments by flight leaders. It's been my experience that the wingmen suffer the consequences of their leader's not so brilliant actions. I don't want to sound callous, but I've seen this happen before and it'll happen again. I don't want to dwell on these mishaps except to learn from them.

"I can't brush his death off as easily as you, Tommy. In my mind, I picture him as a fighter pilot and a young vigorous man whose life has been cut short. I see you as a fighter pilot and realize your flying is dangerous as hell. Yet you go off every day with a smile on your face and a chip on your shoulder to prove what...that you're better than every other fighter pilot in the sky...that you're going to succeed went others fail? Tell me why you act that way, Tommy, so I can understand and enjoy my life with you."

"Honey, I sure didn't have this attitude growing up. It started when they accepted me for flying training. Our instructors told us we were in the upper two percent of all Americans men our age. I believed them. When I was selected for training in fighters the program emphasized the aggressive attitude needed to stay alive in combat. This tiger program convinced me that I was a better pilot than anyone else in the air. The other trainees felt the same way but I knew they were lying to themselves. I believed in me and my actions in the air during the war proved my belief. One doesn't have to fly airplanes to have this attitude. You just have to be tolerant of those not blessed with it. Peggy, does this make any sense?"

"Not right now. I'm going to have to think about what you said. In the meantime, hold me close."

"If you're up to it, we have time for a swim when you finish your baking chore. There's not enough time for me to drive to the base and back before dinner. We can do that tomorrow. We'll go to the chapel on base for Sunday mass and then brunch at the officer's club. I'll be in the back yard cleaning up the car until you're ready. By the way, the gulf's water temperature is just right."

"Hey there Tommy, won't you join us for lunch?" a smiling Amos Jackson called from across the club' dining room His loud voice with a deep Texan accent annoyed some senior officers and their wives. Tommy was greeted by a firm handshake as Amos announced "I'd like to present my wife Tina. We've been married almost two weeks. We met in a road side café near Rose Bud, Texas. I used my best pick up line to get her to dance with me."

"And what were those pearls of wisdom?" asked a smiling Tommy.

Laughing, Amos answered, "I went up to her, and in my sexiest tiger voice, purred, 'will you marry me… while you're thinking that over, dance with me.' After the dance she dragged me over to her daddy and told him I wanted to marry her. Well, he was a rough looking mule skinner, but he smiled through a couple missing teeth and gave us his blessing. You have to admit, Tina is easy on the eyes."

Tommy nodded his agreement and introduced Peggy. The brunch turned into the beginning of a two hour gab fest as Tina and Peggy swapped newlywed news and Tommy and Amos talked about their new assignment.

The tables around them became very quiet as Tommy told Amos about witnessing the crash and his attempt to rescue the pilot. In retelling the story, tears swelled in Peggy's eyes. But before a tear could fall from her gray eyes, a booming voice from a red faced full colonel asked, "Are you Captain Thompson?"

"Yes sir, I am."

"My staff has been looking for you, but your name is not on any of the rosters of any of the base's units. Why in the hell is that so?"

"I just arrived on base this morning and haven't signed in, sir."

"Captain, I'm Colonel Donovan and I'm the President of the accident investigating board for the P-51 crash you witnessed. The accident board meets tomorrow morning at 0900 in my office. You will be there."

"Yes sir," replied Tommy, "But I don't know where your office is located."

Addressing a major standing behind him, the colonel ordered, "Give the captain the information he needs. Ladies, please excuse the interruption… enjoy your lunch," he said with a smile, evaluating the wives with a practiced eye as he turned back to his table.

Tina looked at Peggy and in a soft Texas drawl murmured, "I bet he's a dirt road sport."

Under her breath, Peggy responded, "Us Yankees don't use that term, but I sure as hell know what you mean." Tommy and Amos couldn't figure out why they were giggling.

Standing at the front of the club as they were about to go their separate ways, Peggy pulled Tommy aside and whispered, "Amos and Tina haven't found a place to live. We have extra rooms and if they agree to share the expenses they could stay with us. Tina and I would be good company for each other and if you and Amos drive to work together, us girls would have transportation." Squeezing his hand and pulling him close, she whispered, "Please Tommy."

"Sounds like a good idea only if you put them in bedroom far from ours. You know how loud horny fighter pilots can get. Hey Amos, wait up a second. Peggy has a plan and I have a phone call to make."

Jeremiah greeted the two couples at the front door and, as instructed by Tommy during his telephone call, escorted the Jacksons to a corner bedroom upstairs far from the master bedroom. Amos tried to tip Jeremiah but was taken aback when Jeremiah said, "Captain, a gratuity is not allowed in this house ever, but thank you kindly. I believe Captain and Miz Thompson are going to the beach and asked if you would join them."

"We will, Jeremiah, right after we change." As Jeremiah pulled the door closed, Amos was struggling to pull Tina's skirt down. "Patience Amos, let me undo a couple buttons and hang up the clothes before they get wrinkled." Glancing at his erection, Tina said, "Nevermind."

Chapter 29

Arriving at the colonel's office fifteen minutes early, Tommy was surprised to see Dr. Dan Bowers sitting there twiddling his thumbs. "Captain, I'm happy to see a familiar face. Damn son, those sparklies on your chest indicate you've seen quite a bit of action. You don't appear to be old enough to have a combat record those decorations attest to."

"Well Doctor Dan, sometimes I feel older than the hills, but right now I feel like a virgin interviewing for a job on Post Office Street in Galveston, Texas. I don't know all that's going to happen, but I certainly expect to be screwed."

"Captain, if you tell the truth I'm sure you'll do just fine."

After Tommy's twenty minute eyewitness account of the accident to the board, Colonel Donovan raised up out of his chair, put his hands on the table and hissed through his clenched teeth, "Bullshit Captain, bullshit!"

Tommy's face became bright red as he fought back his anger. After a deep breath he replied in a not so steady voice, "Sir, I swore to tell the truth and I did."

"Captain, your testimony contradicts the testimony of the flight leader. Get out of that chair and wait in the anteroom. Call in the next witness, Dr Dan Bowers."

Tommy passed Dr. Bowers as he went in to the board room and said, "My expectations were exceeded."

In the anteroom was a Lt. Colonel nervously twisting his West Point ring on his finger. Under his pilot wings there was a row of ribbons, none of which indicate service in a war theater. They sat there not saying a word to each other. Fifteen minutes later, Dr. Dan came out, took a business card from his wallet, handed it to Tommy and said, "Call me," and left the building. The Lt. Colonel went into the room and, just as the door closed, the Colonel's loud voice yelled, "You lying son of a bitch, give me those wings."

Five minutes later, an uneasy Tommy was called back into the board room. As he came to attention before the accident board officers, they stood up as one and the presiding board chairman said, "Captain Thompson, I offer you the sincerest apology that I can express. I am embarrassed that a West Point graduate, a group of honorable officers of which I am a member, would lie under oath to save his skin. Again, please accept my apology."

"I accept sir."

"Dismissed."

Christmas Help

Tommy located a telephone and called Dr. Bowers' office. "Tommy I can't believe the horse manure that board was trying to get me to swallow. I told them exactly what I saw, emphasizing your effort to rescue the pilot that they hadn't heard about. Before I left the room, the colonel was about to blow his top. I suggested he settle down before he had a heart attack. Did he?" asked Dr. Bowers.

"No he didn't, but I believe he ended the career of a fellow ring knocker. Doctor, if you and your wife have no plans for dinner tonight, would you join my wife and another couple for dinner?" Tommy offered.

"I know Sarah's cooking and wouldn't pass it up for anything," a delighted doctor agreed.

"Is seven a good time for you?" asked Tommy.

"We'll be there on time. I hope you all have a taste for wine as I have a couple of bottles that would compliment Sarah's cooking."

The Bowers arrived by boat and tied their Criscraft to the dock. Both were tan and athletic looking and when they smiled their white teeth sparkled. They handed Tommy their gift of wine and Jeremiah served all martinis.

"Jeremiah, you haven't lost your touch with the gin and vermouth. As always, they are excellent. A toast to you gentlemen who fly and fight and to their beautiful ladies who put up with their antics. May all your flights have happy landings."

"And a toast to you Doctor, for saving my career. And a toast to your wife. That colonel didn't like my testimony and I feared my flying days were over. Thanks again."

"Ladies and gentlemen, dinner is served," announced Jeremiah.

Awaiting them in the dining room on a large oval oak table was a baked red snapper, oyster stuffing ,three bean salad and hush puppies. A three layer chocolate cake, hidden in the kitchen, rounded off the menu.

"I've taken the liberty of pouring the wine offered by Dr. Bowers. If you need anything, please ring the bells. I'll be in the kitchen with Sarah," Jeremiah said as he excused himself."

"If you ever tire of Sarah and Jeremiah, please call me to pick them up. There are no finer cooks in Florida," pleaded Dan Bower's wife.

"Sorry, but they are on long term contracts with Thompson Industries. Once my dad gets his first taste of Sarah's cooking, he'll make the term a little bit longer," quipped Tommy.

Chapter 30

"Gentlemen, I'm Lt. Colonel Dallas Wren, your commander and project officer for this Top Secret test program. You ten pilots in front of me are reputed to be the best and most experienced fighter pilots that the European Theater of Operations has to offer. I'm an aeronautical engineer with seventy five missions in P-51's and my claim to fame is I was shot down by a German ME-262. Never saw it coming and only had a glimpse of it from my parachute as he left the area. The project you are here for will, hopefully, put us on an even playing field with any air power that has jet propelled aircraft."

"We have jet propelled aircraft?' a wide eyed Amos asked.

"Yes, we do. There are only sixteen in existence in the United States and four of them are here at Eglin. They're on the far side of the field. We keep them in a large hanger out of view to the public."

"What do you call these beauties?" a deep voiced captain asked, exhaling cigar smoke through his nose.

"They're called the P-80 Shooting Star. Believe me when I say they live up to their name. You'll all get eight hours of ground school on this beast and then four one hour sorties for familiarization. After your introductory flights, the fun will begin. I say fun, even though there's a lot of paper work associated with each flight. Since you are all captains, I'll select who flies first in the most democratic manner I know."

"Is there anyone here from the great state of Texas?"

Amos raised his hand.

"You're first, partner. I understand from looking over your records that we have a German ace in our group. Captain Thompson, would you explain how you gained this title?"

"First, I was never shot down by an enemy fighter. My magnet ass seemed to attract ground fire from those troops that were engaged in battles with the allied forces. My good luck prevailed because I crashed near allied personnel who helped me avoid being captured."

"Thompson, you'll be second to fly."

"Thank you, sir. I knew my magnet ass would hold me in good stead with this distinguished group of intrepid flyboys." The gathering responded well to Tommy's smart ass remark considering they were green with envy at not being selected first or second.

"You people are supposed to be the best there were in Europe. I hope that you all had victories over the Luftwaffe, otherwise I'm briefing the wrong group. Let's see

Christmas Help

the hands of those who shot down at least one of the bad guys."

All raised a hand.

"I'll put the rest of you on the roster according to the number of missions you have flown, which, by the way, are less than the total that the number one and two selected had flown. If you'll follow me out to our bus, we'll go and give this sweet machine the once over. You may touch it but please, drooling is not allowed when you sit in the cockpit."

Three of the P-80's had scaffolding around them while the fourth had it's tail feathers removed, revealing a General Electric J33-9 engine. "That little thing is going to push us around the sky," exclaimed Amos.

"Yes it will, and at over 500 miles an hour. There are some newer engines coming that the manufacturers say will push it to 600 mph," replied Wren. "If you'll break into groups of three and gather around the other aircraft, three of our instructor pilots will attempt to amaze you with their vast knowledge of the aircraft which has been gained in the last week. They have each had three rides in the machine and have probably made as many mistakes as a pilot can make and still be alive. Their bad experiences will keep you from making the same ones. Captain Jackson, I'll escort you so that I can practice my Texas drawl on you. Gentlemen, your learning curve on this machine will be a sharp climbing line. If you get behind the "curve" you won't be in this program long. There are no dumb questions…and hopefully no dumb answers…so ask away. We'll be here for three hours, then to lunch at the snack bar and then we're off to ground school."

Driving out the front gate on the way home that evening, Tommy remarked to Amos, "I think I'm going to like being part of this project. The pace seems a little bit fast and I wonder what he has in mind after we get our four orientation rides out of the way."

"It has to be dog fighting. That is the impression I have in my little old cotton picking head, Tommy."

"Maybe Amos, because several in our class have been shot down, they're looking for cannon fodder…that's just the devil advocate in me speaking. Hell, let's just roll with the punches and enjoy the opportunity to go balls out in that pretty looking thing. Speaking of pretty looking things, I'm sorry we won't be able to tell the wives about our job. Let's tell them we'll be flying the P-51. I don't like lying to Peggy but it beats telling her the project is classified. She would screw me to death to get that secret past my lips. Does that sound like the way to go?"

"Tell her it's classified…I like that part where she's screwing you to death," Amos said quickly. "But I can't think of a better plan other than a little white lie. What do you think the girls did today other than spend our hard earned money?"

"Peggy mentioned they were going to the officer's club for lunch. Then to the base commissary for staples that Sarah needed for the kitchen. She also said if the steaks looked good, she would get a couple for dinner. We'll split the cost, unless you are hard up for money then it'll be my treat."

"Tommy, I'm going to tell you something that I don't want you to share with anyone…not even Peggy."

"Don't tell me you have another wife."

"Worse than that."

"You got the clap."

"No, absolutely not."

"Well I give up. What is this dark secret?"

"You promise not to tell anyone…especially Tina?"

"Yes I promise. Now, damn it, tell me."

"I'm one rich son of a bitch."

"I think you've been out in the sun too long, Amos. Rich my ass."

"Well, I am. My granddaddy left me a section of land out in west Texas when he died. The family thought it was payback for all the nasty tricks I played on him as a kid. He and I were really thick back then…laughing and scratching… and both of us getting whacked by granny when we got crossways with her. He gave me my first taste of whiskey when I was twelve. I can still feel that burning in my throat. When I was fourteen, we went to the red light district in El Paso to get me an education from some pretty understanding ladies. For my sixteenth birthday, there was a World War one Jenny sitting in the north forty that he paid a hundred dollars for. The pilot that flew it to the ranch gave me ten minutes of instructions, helped me start it, and I was off and flying. Didn't know what in the hell I was doing, but I was flying. My only mistake was buzzing granny as she was hanging out the laundry. I came a little too close and she peed in her drawers. It took all of forty acres and Granny's garden to land that thing. Granny was there to greet me with a switch when I turned the magnetos off. Her present for my sixteenth birthday was sixteen good licks and one to grow on. Granddad also got a good lick with that switch before he grabbed Granny and gave her a smooch that got both of them laughing. Damn, I miss that old coot."

"So how does one square mile of parched dirt growing cactus translate into making you rich?"

"Well, this oil exploration company came by and started to drill for that black liquid gold and, sure enough, they found it. Actually, they found it seventeen times. My royalty checks make my eyes water every three months."

"So you're rich. Why don't you want Tina to know about your good fortune?"

"Because I don't believe she knows how to manage money and I think she would go hog wild finding ways to spend it. So please don't tell her."

"Okay, I promise."

Parking the car in the rear of the house, they spotted the girls unloading the groceries. "Hey, we'll help you with that," Tommy called out.

"Thanks, and there's some mail in there someplace,"

Tina replied. "Amos, I opened some of yours by mistake. I hope you don't mind...I thought they were from some old girl friend but they were just from some rinky-dink bank in Odessa stating they deposited your royalty checks. The numbers on them are almost as big as the ones I get."

"Almost as big as mine? Honey, you're rich?"

"Yes, I am. I didn't want to tell you for fear that you would want to spend some of it on foolish things we don't need."

"Why are you getting royalty checks? You told me your daddy was a mule skinner."

"He was when he worked the fields around Petrolia. He took a chance on drilling one for himself. He went into debt hat, ass and spurs and lucked out on his first attempt. He didn't need any fancy equipment to find the next holes. He used a witch stick from a Mesquite tree... walked around with it in his two hands until it bent down to the earth and then he drilled in that spot. He did good, I mean, Texas good. He gave me an oil well every year on my birthday since I was ten. Then the boom went bust. It's a good thing the wells were in my name because he lost everything he owned betting on card games. I put him on an allowance that let's him get drunk, naked and howl at the moon once a month. He was sober the night you kinda proposed. He knew I wanted you."

"Tina, you are my kind of girl. Granny told me you were a keeper."

"Will you rich people stop counting your money and blessings so that dinner can get started. By the way guys, how was your first day with the P-80?" queried Peggy.

"That, my dear, is supposed to be one damn big secret. Where in the hell did you pick up that tidbit of information?"

"At the officers club. The wives were having a luncheon and invited Tina and me to join them. The table we were at had three ladies our age, who told us their husbands were instructor pilots on some hush-hush project. We told them you guys were fighter pilots back from Europe for some classified thing. They told us, in the strictest of confidence of course, that you two would be flying a jet propelled aircraft called the P-80. Gosh Tommy, won't that be dangerous?"

"Not really. But your comments seem to verify that old saw on spreading the news quickly…telegraph, telephone or tell an officer's wife. Ladies, please don't tell anyone else or Amos and I are going to be in big trouble," begged Tommy

"Well if your good old boys' club wants to keep this a secret, then a secret it'll be. But you have to teach us the secret handshake," Tina said laughing.

"Tommy and I will be holding that class tonight in the bedrooms," promised Amos.

Chapter 31

"Gentlemen, you've completed the ground school with no written test score less than 98%. Seems none of you remembered my serial number. Captains Jackson and Thompson will be first in the air this morning. When you two are in the number one position, the instructors will climb the ladder the crew chief left on the canopy rail. With your brakes full on, run your engine up to 100%. The instructor will point at the gauges and give you a thumbs up or down. After his thumbs up, retard the throttle and he will get off the aircraft, taking the ladder with him. Remember to close and lock the damn canopy. When the tower clears you two for take off and after you get airborne, you two will become members in a very prestigious group called jet fighter pilots. One of the instructor pilots will chase your flight in a P-51 and will be available on the briefed radio frequency in case you need help." Lt. Col. Wren concluded with, "Good luck and enjoy."

Amos, with Tommy in close formation, radioed "Gear up." With wheels in the well, he called "Flaps." Smoothly the flaps retracted to the up position but the two aircraft remained at tree top level until his speed hit 400 mph. Then, with just a wee bit of back pressure on the stick, Amos was climbing straight up doing aileron rolls. Right next to him was Tommy doing barrel rolls around Amos' aircraft.

"Okay you two, impressive as that tiger exit out of traffic was, settle down to the briefed mission," radioed the chase pilot.

"Hey Tommy, the girls said they would be sunbathing and since the house is along the route to the practice area, let's say hello."

"Just one little hello sounds right," agreed Tommy

"That's not on the mission checklist," interjected the chase pilot.

After the "hello," they preformed all the required maneuvers and on the way back to the field they flew a circular "good bye" at three hundred feet that brought the two topless, sunbathing wives to their feet. Waving the top half of their swimming suits to their wide eyed husbands, they didn't realize that the chase pilot also possessed twenty-twenty vision.

"Hey Amos, slow that thing down and let's take another look at our sweethearts. They look remarkably healthy, those pair."

"Both pairs look healthy to me."

"Nice tits," commented the chase pilot.

"If you were a gentleman you'd've closed your eyes."

"I kept one eye closed. Does that count?"

"Enough of the burlesque show…let's head for base."

Their perfect three touch and go landings almost brought a smile to Lt. Col. Wren's face, who remarked to one of his instructor pilots, "Those two are going to be stiff competition for our so called "Aces Over" group. Let's get the next two airborne…only tell them I want 30 seconds interval between takeoffs."

The maintenance crews swarmed over the returning aircraft and had them serviced and ready for the next crews in thirty minutes. The aircraft performed flawlessly and the ground crews tirelessly. The pilots on the other hand acted less professionally as they tried every maneuver they had learned in their combat tours. One pilot did an eight point roll above the tree tops through a forest fire in the Choctawatchee National Forest. There was no one there to witness this feat except some brown bears and the chase pilot, who kept saying, "You're not really going to do what I think you're going to do…damn that was pretty. Now knock it off!"

The three o'clock thunderstorms were right on schedule as the last man completed his landing roll. Two hours of paper work and debriefing fleshed out the rest of the day. The pilots gathered at the officers' stag bar to toast their status as jet fighter pilots. In keeping with their image as egotistical, self centered, death defying, daring individuals, their toast rang through out the bar:

Here's to me in my sober moods when I ramble, sit and think,

And here's to me in my drunken moods when I gamble, screw and drink.

And when these moods are over and from this world I pass,

I hope they bury me upside down,

So the world can kiss my ass.

At the end of July, all pilots had completed the required flights. The only incident occurred during a landing roll in the middle of a thunderstorm. A steady crosswind blew one of the instructor pilot's aircraft off the runway. The only damage was his pride.

"Amos, we've been at this for almost a month now and I don't know when I have enjoyed flying this much," Tommy remarked as he set his lemonade glass down on the porch steps.

"They have thrown every type of aircraft the Army has in its inventory against us during the dog fighting sessions. And old buddy, you and I have waxed each and every one of them. I believe I told you, not so long ago, one hazy day over France, that we were good and sure enough we are," a suntanned Amos replied.

"Two of our classmates were eliminated… neither one had one "kill" in ten engagements. That surprised me. I can't understand how they got so disoriented out over the water," wondered Tommy. "When they took that half second to 'right' their bodies' gyro, the bad guys had them. Hey, better them than us. Pass the pitcher and let's drink to tomorrow's briefing. Wren said he had a surprise for us."

"Okay you two aces," Peggy called, "…dinner is on the table."

* * *

"I told you we should have let those instructor pilots win at least one of those two versus two dog fighting sorties," whispered Tommy.

"We're not of that mind set, Tommy. Probably never will be," replied Amos.

"Take a seat you two hot rocks. First, congratulations on polishing off every one of my instructors including two Aces. They came down from those flights so damn mad that they threw their helmets against the wall and shattered them. And you two didn't help them get over their frustrations by coming into the debriefing room laughing and scratching like some ranch hands visiting Grandma's whore house for the first time."

"We could tell them we're sorry if you think that would sooth their ruffled feathers," offered Tommy.

"Perhaps a discussion on basic acrobatics would help them as they seem to prefer the Lufbery as the only way to wage war in a three dimension environment," suggested Amos.

"Enough! You two will remain here for the next seven days. You can brush up on your flying skills before you are sent to the next phase of this test program. You can fly any of the aircraft on our line, except the P-80's, and if the spirit moves you, take them cross country. No restrictions. Just don't get hurt because your classmates will all be on their way to their next duty stations and we won't have a replacement for you. Report back here on the fifth of August at 0700 hours ready to fly. Bring your shaving kit, an extra flying suit and underwear. Tell your wives you will be back in a week. If you have questions, save them, because I don't have the answers. Dismissed"

They returned the main gate guard's salute and for one minute there was silence as they started the trip home. "Amos, let's take a couple of T-6's over to Montgomery for lunch tomorrow."

"Won't the wives be just a little unhappy? We're going to be gone a week and to take a weekend cross country will really pissed them off," a surprised Amos answered.

"Not when we tell them they're going with us."

"Obviously you have a plan."

"As a matter of fact I do, and it'll work, trust me, it'll work."

The Buick came to a stop next to Jeremiah working in the garden. "Jeremiah, would you please take the tractor with the mowing attachment and cut the weeds down to three inches? Make a swath 75 feet wide by two thousand feet long."

"Captain, if you're going to bring an aircraft in here

like the previous owner's son occasionally did, then I know exactly where to start."

"Will you be able to finish it today, Jeremiah?"

"I'll have it done by dinner, Captain."

The wives were more than excited and screamed with delight. The first question was, "What do we wear?"

Tommy's answered, "I have two of the smallest flying suits I could scrounge in the trunk of the car. There are also two head sets so we can talk to each other. Pack a skirt, blouse and some lipstick."

"What if someone asks us what we're doing in the army's airplanes? Any ideas on an answer?" Peggy asked.

"Tell them you're hitching a ride to California to ferry an aircraft," offered Amos. "Big lies are easier to swallow if you smile."

Peggy and Tina were sitting under an oak tree, sipping lemonade, when two T-6 aircraft landed and taxied to them. While the dust settled, Jeremiah showed the ladies how to put the homemade chocks in front and behind the wheels, avoiding the spinning propeller. Tommy and Amos deplaned and strapped their wives in the back seat. Back in the cockpit with his headset on, Tommy could hear Peggy breathing deeply. "Peggy, sweetheart, are you sure you want to do this?"

"Hell yes I do. This is going to be better than the roller coaster at the Dane county fair."

Jeremiah removed the chocks, Tommy advanced the throttle and, in what seemed like a life time of bouncing and skipping to Peggy, they were airborne. Amos and Tina stayed in loose formation as both pilots allowed the ladies to handle the control stick.

"Hey Amos, how's she doing?"

"The aircraft and Tina are doing great. She says she's going to take flying lessons first chance she gets. How about your sweetie?"

"I think we've created a monster. She won't give me control of the aircraft back. So sit back and relax… she'll follow the coast line over to Montgomery."

"Tommy, I want to try a stall."

"That's easy. Just pull back on the stick and throttle while you keep putting in right rudder. Stop putting in rudder when the aircraft starts to shake. Keep the wings level. You're doing great, honey. Whoops! Too much rudder. I got the controls now until I get us out of this spin. If you want to, follow me through with your hands and feet lightly on the controls." The spin recovery wasn't that difficult and, after two turns, they were climbing back towards Montgomery.

"Tommy, let me do that again. I love the way the earth was spinning, blurring all the greens and browns together…and those shadows racing across the cockpit. The engine noise…wow, rumbling then screaming… what a sensual feeling. That feeling was right up there next to sex."

"Really, just like sex?"

"No silly, I said up there next to sex."

"Tommy, is there anything wrong with your aircraft?"

"No Amos, we're just having a sex education session. Okay Peggy. just one more only this time we'll let it spin three times."

The spin and shaking were a little more intense, and Peggy's screams of delight made Tommy wonder how in he hell could he top this experience in the bedroom.

"I'll take us in for a landing at that airstrip off our left wing tip."

The landing on the dirt strip and the taxiing to a restaurant next to a golf course had dust rolling across the empty eighteenth green. "Amos do you see that B-25 parked under the trees?"

"Sure do partner. I don't know what to make of it, but it's too late to worry about it. It's here and so are we."

Tommy held the brakes as Peggy found some chocks and placed them against the wheels. Tina followed the routine as good as any line rat could do. With the aircraft between them and the restaurant, the ladies slipped out of the coveralls and into their dresses.

Amos interrupted Tommy filling out the aircraft logs. "Partner, you're missing one of the prettiest sights in Alabama. And to think we're the lucky bastards that will sleep with them tonight."

"I hope you mean you with your wife and me with mine. You're right...in their bras and panties they make those magnolia blossoms look faded."

Out of the corner of her eye, Tina caught them looking and nudged Peggy. "I think we're going to have our hands full tonight."

Glancing over the fuselage, Peggy giggled, "Well let's wiggle our behinds a little more and make sure."

Arm in arm and smiling like a bunch of school kids, they made their way to the restaurant entrance that was blocked by a familiar senior officer.

"Just what in the hell do you folks think you are doing?" the red faced accident board president, Colonel Donovan, quietly demanded through clenched teeth. A vein was pulsating in his red neck.

"Colonel we dropped in for lunch," explained Tommy, not giving any more information than requested.

"And who are those two ladies?"

"They're our wives, sir."

"Do you know how many regulations you two have broken?"

"No sir, we don't."

Before the colonel could enumerate them, a shapely, long legged young blonde came up and grabbed his arm, purring, "Darling, our lunch is getting cold. Can't this wait?"

Blushing a brighter red, the colonel quietly continued, "Gentlemen, your indiscretion and mine are best forgotten. Enjoy your lunch."

"A table for four, far from that good looking blonde," Tommy requested of the hostess.

Pretending to look over the menu Tommy noted, "What we've seen and heard here is now a closely guarded secret. Everybody agree?"

"We agree that that blonde was not the colonel's wife. I reckon the secret handshake isn't necessary to seal our lips," Tina nonchalantly uttered, batting her eyelashes.

"I don't know," giggled Peggy, "that blonde doesn't look like the handshake type to me."

"Before this gets out of hand, so to speak, shall we order lunch?" suggested Amos.

Chapter 32

"The brass couldn't have picked a nicer day to send us to fly to Yuma, Arizona, Tommy. Not a cloud in the sky," Amos radioed from his P-47 as they taxied into their parking spots.

"They certainly couldn't have picked a hotter one. It has to be at least a hundred and ten, and I don't see any thing that looks like a shade tree. Even with this four bladed prop churning, my flight suit is soaking wet," Tommy observed as sweat rolled off his ears.

The operations shack really was a dilapidated wooden shack. Major Bernade, standing in what little shade the building offered, said, "Gentlemen, welcome to our small patch of Dante's inferno. Why didn't you plan to arrive in the morning and save us all from the heat? We try to get our flying out of the way in the cool of the morning," Bernade noted as perspiration trickled off his forehead. "Which one of you is Thompson?"

"I am sir. Our orders were to get here as quickly as possible. Sorry for the inconvenience."

"I'm usually not this surly, Thompson , but this ramp temperature is over one hundred and thirty and I need a drink. Come with me. I've got a few long necks in a pail of ice in the station wagon. I'll show you where your bunks are. I'll brief you on tomorrow's mission at breakfast. Help yourself to a beer."

That ice cold brew did much to improve everyone's attitude. "I didn't see anything that looked like a permanent structure for the bachelor officers' quarters," Amos remarked as he rolled the cold wet bottle across his forehead. Even with the windows open, the hundred plus wind temperature was quickly melting the ice in the bucket.

"Captain, the only permanent structure on this air patch is the hanger where a couple of P-80's are parked. Tent city is where you can bunk and get out of the sun."

"Tent city? Isn't there anything like a motel or hotel in town?" Tommy asked.

"One motel, one restaurant and one blinking traffic light make up downtown Yuma. The motel is expensive, but each room has a swamp cooler. They have a swimming pool about the size of a postage stamp if you like water warmer than piss. Anyway, you haven't been authorized per diem so it looks like the tents will have to do. Let's have another round while the beer is still cold."

Tommy used the GI can opener that hung around his neck with his dog tags and popped the lids on three bottles. Handing them to appreciative hands, he inquired, "Can you loan us some transportation for our stay here?"

"Best I can do is a pickup truck."

"Amos, do you want tent or town?"

"Town, and it'll be my treat."

His answer shocked the field grade officer. "Captain, are you rich?"

"No sir, but my wife is."

The steak at the restaurant was, in Tommy's words, "...a little tough but tasty and the sixteen ounce size was a suitable substitute for the lack of flavor." The motel room's swamp cooler was noisy but neither Tommy nor Amos had any trouble sleeping because they finished off half a case of Mexican beer sitting poolside. Driving out to the air field the next morning at 04:30, a yawning Amos remarked, "The morning temperature is almost chilly. Let's spend tonight in the tents. It can't be all that bad."

"I'm all for it. That scorpion I had to share the shower with looked mean as hell to me," Tommy replied.

"*I wasn't exactly crazy about his curled tail*," Bartholomew confessed.

They found the mess hall in a Quonset hut at the end of a dusty road. The eggs and biscuits with beef and gravy were almost running off the metal tray. "If you gentlemen would join Major Bernade out on the patio, I'll bring some coffee and juice out to you," a rather large sergeant dressed in cut off olive drab trousers and "T" shirt politely offered. A ragged scar on his muscular left arm bisected the tattooed heart with Mother lettered on it, ensured no one was going to criticized his culinary talents.

"Good morning, gentlemen."

"Good morning, Major. We put a few bottles of beer in your station wagon as token of our appreciation for your hospitality and generosity."

"Thanks. Hope you slept well, because you'll have to be bright eyed and bushy tailed for this morning's mission. Take off is at oh six thirty. The P-80's will have a full internal fuel and auxiliary tanks. There will be no armament on board, just wing cameras. You'll proceed to a point one hundred ten miles northeast at twenty thousand feet. At this point, a simulated enemy flight of two will challenge you from your 12 o'clock position and the fight begins. Your call sign will be Candy."

"Who's our enemy and what will they be flying?" asked Tommy.

"Messerschmitt ME-262's piloted by two of our Navy's aces. Their call sign will be Fearless. They will be flying out of a classified location. Do not, I repeat do not follow them as they recover at that base. That is all the mission information I can give you. Any questions?"

"Where did the ME-262's come from?" asked Tommy.

"They were liberated from the Messerschmitt factory, shipped through the port in Houston, then trucked to their present location. They have been here about six weeks.

Today, August sixth, will be the first encounter of this jet against an American jet."

"Sounds like a piece of cake," Amos said, chomping at the bit.

"Sounds like a trap to me," Tommy said under his breath.

During the preflight, Tommy pulled Amos aside. "Partner, this whole set-up stinks. First off, we'll still have fuel in the tip tanks when the engagement starts. This extra fuel will slow our rate of roll and acceleration, putting us at a distinct disadvantage…and why did they want us at twenty thousand feet? There's nothing more useless than sky above you or runway behind you. Let's take them up to thirty thousand then drop the tanks when we spot them. Do you see a flaw in my thinking?"

"The only problem I see is that we're going to piss off whoever dreamed up this party. But as a fighter pilot, I'm not in favor of being a clay pigeon at someone's airborne skeet range. Let's have at them with our cameras rolling. Kill 'em with film is as good as it is going to get and you and I are going to click them good."

"Candy Two, I have contrails twelve o'clock high about forty miles."

"Tommy, those sons of bitches are at thirty five thousand. You were right about this being a trap.'

"Amos, throttle to one hundred per cent. Holler when you see the bandits."

"Tallyho lead."

"Roger that. I have a visual. A lazy chandelle should put us in their six o'clock position. We'll stay out of the contrail altitude until we have them by the short hairs. Pickle the drop tanks…now! Change to the mission frequency."

"Two is on."

"Lead is on. Good morning, Fearless enemy," a confident Tommy transmitted.

"What's your position Candy ass flight?" an arrogant, impatient voice answered as he banked his aircraft sharply left and right looking for his prey.

"Try six o'clock, one hundred feet and consider yourself dead meat. Want to try and get rid of us?"

The ME-262's pilots immediately rolled their aircraft over and pointed them at the desert floor. From thirty five thousand feet down to the valley floor, using every evasive action they knew, they tried to shed Tommy and Amos but to no avail. Engine power varied from 100 percent to idle with dive brakes extended then retracted as the four aircraft twisted and barrel rolled, dodging cacti and rock formations. Six G pull ups followed by zero G inverted flight couldn't shake Candy flight. Fuel monitoring was left unattended until an exasperated and furious lead ME-262 pilot transmitted, "We have a low fuel warning light, going to tower frequency."

"Tommy it's pucker time…I'm down to fifty gallons. Not enough for the trip back," Amos said uneasily.

Tommy didn't believe Amos at first. His fuel totalizer read two hundred and thirty gallons remaining. His

Christmas Help

stomach tightened and a silent "oh shit' passed his lips as he remembered he didn't reset the damn thing when he jettisoned the tip tanks. He mentally chastised himself when his low fuel light illuminated. His heart was beating a bit faster as he realized his options to keep from bailing out or crashing were limited to violating an order. Of greater concern, he put his wing man in jeopardy. Sloppy leadership…I could use a little luck to get out of this mess I put us in.

That's why I'm here. Get your head out of your ass and latch on to your fleeing foe, suggested Bartholomew.

"Same fuel state here, Amos…I guess we're going to have to do the big no-no." He brought his flight in echelon formation with the ME-262's and pitched out to land at the classified base. The tower's frantic warnings not to land were ignored and he parked his flight's aircraft next to the ME-262's.

"Candy two, what's your fuel state?"

"Lead, I show ten gallons. Looks like we came out even…out of fuel and out of the blue."

This was supposed to be a lark. A pleasant interlude from war. These two keep an angel busy, Bartholomew thought, putting the luck back in the bag.

Tommy was amazed at the physical layout of the airbase. The runway and ramp blended into the desert so well that if they hadn't latched onto the ME-262 for landing, he would have been hard pressed to find this place.

If there were buildings on this piece of desert, he sure as hell couldn't spot them.

"You smart asses are in deep shit not only for landing here, but for not flying the briefed mission," a frustrated naval aviator shouted as he met up with Tommy.

Inserting himself between the two flight commanders, Amos ordered, "Get out of my leader's face."

A push from one of the Navy's finest was retaliated with a Texas round house punch that sunk the Annapolis graduate.

"You can't treat a Navy Aviator like that," a Fearless wingman yelled. His punch closed to its intended target but missed because Amos ducked and Tommy didn't. He fell on top of Fearless one as he was getting to his knees. Tommy grabbed Amos' leg and managed to trip him and his opponent.

The fight continued with all involved rolling on the hot tarmac until a military policeman fired a couple of rounds from his 45 caliber pistol into the air. "Gentlemen, gentlemen, the group commander wanted to see just the intruders until the fight broke out. Now he would like a word with all of you. Please wipe the blood off your faces. Try to remember you're officers and gentlemen. I'll drive you to the officers' club."

"They have an officer's club? Just where in the hell is it?" Before anyone could answer Tommy's question, a sizable chunk of mountain moved sideways, allowing two tugs to pull the Me-262's into the cave. The police vehicle followed them into the tremendous cavern, stopping short of the giant elevator that took the aircraft down and out of sight.

"This one may be bigger than the one at Carlsbad." Amos remarked. "Not as cool and definitely not as humid."

"I bet a swamp cooler isn't keeping this place comfortable," Tommy conceded, noting that the interior was manmade with steel beams and concrete. All the lights were recessed and placed so there were no shadows.

"Gentlemen, watch your step…the ramp to the elevators is a little dark."

"How many floors does this place have?" asked Amos

"If we told you that, we'd have to keep you here as part of our slave labor contingent," answered the naval aviator with the black eye."

"Yeah," answered his wing man. "And you'll be wearing bell bottoms."

The air policeman grabbed Tommy's arm halfway to its goal…an already bruised chin. "Will you four knock it off…our intruders are smart enough to see there our six buttons to choose from." The door opened at level three, revealing a large room that was decorated as if it belonged in the Waldorf Astoria Hotel.

The dusty and dirty foursome were ushered inside just as the officers' mess was called to attention. Tommy whispered to Amos, "This is the first time I've seen this many enlisted men, civilians, both men and women in an officers' club. Wipe the blood off your cheek, Amos."

"You have a trickle of red stuff coming from your nose, and I don't think it's snot, Tommy."

"At ease," the base commander ordered. "I wanted all personnel presented when I read this press release from the White House entitled, A Statement by the President of the United States."

A hush settled over a surprised crowd.

"Sixteen hours ago, an American airplane dropped one bomb on Hiroshima, Japan and destroyed its usefulness to the enemy. That bomb had more power than 20,000 tons of T.N.T. It had more than two thousand times the blast power of the British "Grand Slam" which is the largest bomb ever yet used in the history of warfare."

A loud chorus of cheers, yelling and whistling drowned out the commander's following remarks until the group sergeant major yelled, "Knock it off."

"Stand at ease while I finish one more paragraph. 'It is an atomic bomb. It is a harnessing of the basic power of the universe The force from which the sun draws its power has been loosed against those who brought war to the Far East.' President Truman's statement goes on to describe historical events leading up to the production of the bomb. I'll have copies of the president's statement posted on every bulletin board in the cave.

"It is hoped that this action will destroy the Japanese will to continue war. All activities scheduled for today are cancelled. Those of you that are so inclined may go to the chapel and thank God that this event will save countless American lives. The rest of you may partake in a free happy hour. You pilots," his crooked finger pointing at the bruised, battered and dirty foursome, "follow me to the club manager's office."

The mad dash to the bar almost trampled those who were standing contemplating the consequences of the dropped bomb. With all the cheering and laughter surrounding those few individuals, the sober thoughts of unforeseen consequences were lost.

The door slammed as the steady, disgusted voice of the group commander continued, "If I wasn't so fucking happy about the dropping of the bomb I'd cashier you all out of the service for conduct unbecoming an officer and make you all walk home. You two Navy aces have been a thorn in my side ever since you arrived here. If I hear another chorus of "Anchors Aweigh" during the remainder of your stay here, I'll personally drive you to the desert and let you serenade the rattlesnakes. Get out of here and join the troops at the bar."

The door closed quietly as he continued cheerfully, "Well, who won the dog fight?"

"We did sir."

"Splendid. Fair and square?"

"Not exactly, sir."

"Makes no difference. A win is a win. You were told not to land here…is that correct?" the Colonel allowed his voice to slip into an annoyed voice of authority.

"Yes sir."

"Tell me why in the hell you did, and it better be a damn good reason."

"After all that chasing around on the deck, getting some mighty fine pictures of ME-262's tail pipes in-between the cacti, we flat didn't have enough fuel to return to our air patch. I've lost one wingman in combat due to ground fire and I wasn't going to lose one today due to my stupidity. It was my decision, sir."

"Thompson, owning up to that major breach of security saved your ass from a letter of reprimand. If you had offered some lame excuse I would have been greatly disappointed and acted much differently. Your airplanes have been refueled and you two will depart posthaste. Most importantly, I want your word that you will not reveal that this facility exists to any one…especially your wives."

"You have our word, Colonel," came the reply from two visibly relieved fighter jocks.

"One last item…this test project has been cancelled by the War Department. Pick up your P-47's at Yuma and return to Eglin. Dismissed! Now get off my dung hill!"

The P-47's engines screamed as they flew inverted over the company's house at Destin, Florida. "That looks like my father's Cadillac parked by front door. I wonder what he's up to," Tommy's voice crackled in Amos' headset.

Working hard to keep his aircraft in tight formation, "He probably drove down to collect the rent money," a flippant Amos suggested.

"We'll find out soon enough. Over to tower and we'll put these beauties on the ramp."

The ground crew had the chocks in place and Tommy had pulled the throttle to the off position when he noticed Lt. Col. Wren waiting in his jeep for them.

"Amos, I hate it when a commander meets me at the aircraft. But he doesn't look too agitated. Perhaps we'll get an "at-a-boy" for waxing those lads from canoe university."

"Don't forget it only takes one "oh shit" to wipe out a hundred "at-a-boys" fearless leader and landing at that classified location might very well be that one " oh shit"" a pessimistic Amos volunteered.

"Welcome back. I understand that you two broke every parameter of the mission briefing, waxed your opponents and somehow a cable from the commander of a classified location gave you two a "well done." It must be the relaxing of tensions after the second super bomb was dropped on Nagasaki, Japan this morning, creating massive casualties. Jump in. I'll take you over to the personal equipment shop to drop off your flying gear and then you can take the rest of the day off."

"That isn't necessary, sir…we can walk."

"Captains, get in the jeep. Time's a wasting. You'll need the rest of the day to get your class "A" uniforms ready for the big parade and awards ceremony tomorrow."

"You mean we're going to have a parade to celebrate the Air Corps wiping out two Japanese cities?" A wide eyed Tommy remarked.

"No, damn it. You two are going to be decorated by a three star general for some deeds you accomplished in Europe. I took the liberty of calling your father, Captain Thompson, and your grandmother, Captain Jackson. I've been told they're at your quarters in Destin. Just how big is that beach house you're renting, anyhow?"

"Between the two houses, there are nine bedrooms," Tommy sheepishly replied.

"Must keep your wife busy sweeping up the sand."

"No sir, the house came with some domestic help."

"Unbelievable. Captain," Lt. Col Wren said, wiping his forehead with his handkerchief, "Be at the officer's club at 0800 with your families. A short coffee and cake meeting with the general and selected staff members will take place. I'll give a quick briefing on the seating plan and your positions on the reviewing stand. At 0850 we will depart for the reviewing stand by bus and at 0900 the ceremony will begin."

"Isn't this a little grand just to pin a couple DFC's on us?" A confused Amos questioned.

"It appears that you Captain Jackson will be awarded a Silver Star and you, Captain Thompson, will be presented the Distinguished Service Cross and a Silver Star."

Tommy's mouth dropped open, his eyes opened wide and stuttered as he politely asked, "Colonel you're kidding, right?"

"Captain, I've been scurrying around this base for two days coordinating this event. I've jumped through more hoops, and made hundreds of phone calls. No, by God, I am not shitting you. You two will be decorated…and you damn well better be on time, sober and spiffy as a shiny new dime."

The drive out to the beach house was a quiet one. Then, suddenly, Amos shouted aloud "yippee ki oh" that startled Tommy out of his daydream of a battle, not so long ago along the Rhine River. "Partner I believe the Army Air Corp has finally realized how important our service has been. We might even get a promotion out of this."

"I don't think so. I believe this is just an excuse to get a lieutenant general out of his office. You know old buddy that you and I are two very fortunate troops."

"You got that right. I don't know where our luck comes from…"

I'd love to tell you, but my instructions have my lips sealed, Bartholomew sighed.

"We've taken more hits than I care to recall, and yet we're here while others who've taken one golden BB are now fertilizing some European farmland. I'll cherish those decorations in remembrance of all our friends who lie under the fields of white crosses throughout Europe."

"Hey, our mood is getting to be a much too somber, Tommy. Let's lighten up… our welcoming committee is sitting on the back porch and they are all smiles."

A sunburned senior Thompson was the first to speak. "I brought Peggy's mom and dad with me. We've been wondering about this house and if it was working out for you. Obviously it has. When Lt. Col. Wren invited me down for the awards ceremony, I thought they might enjoy the sunshine and a look at how their tax dollars have been spent. We picked up Grandma Jackson at the bus station early this morning.

"Well Amos, don't just stand with your mouth open… give your granny a hug."

"I didn't think you'd be up to that long bus ride," he whispered, hugging her frail bones gently.

"Riding wasn't that hard…hard was walking from St. Louis to west Texas behind those covered wagons. It seems like that journey was yesterday."

"She sure is a wonderful lady, full of great stories about West Texas at the turn of the century. Those early Texans certainly were a strong willed group of pioneers," interrupted old man Thompson.

"Is that your nice way of saying I have more crap in me than the Christmas turkey, young man?"

"No offense meant, Mrs. Jackson…let me freshen up your glass of gin."

"I'll get that, Dad."

"Thanks, son. You know Tommy, Tina and Peggy are acting like sisters. I guess it's because the experiences they've shared with you two fly boys. They had us a bit anxious telling us about the flight to Montgomery. I'm surprised you two were able to land those T-6's here and at that golf course without getting a reprimand."

Handing Grandma Jackson a very cold glass of gin Tommy replied, "Landing here was just like landing at the auxiliary strips we used in our primary training. And once that long legged blonde hooked on to the colonel's arm, we were home free."

"Actually, we're all a little jealous that we weren't here to tag along. And your wives didn't mention the colonel's blonde friend. It appears that officers' wives know how to keep secrets."

Amos and Tommy almost choked with laughter when they heard that remark.

"Did I say something funny, boys? Regardless, you know this house is truly a home full of love. Sarah and Jeremiah have made everyone comfortable and we agree that I would give them a bonus for the extra work we have loaded on them. The vote was six to zero."

After an hour of catching up on the news, Tommy and Amos went over the protocol for the next morning. Suddenly Mary realized they were going to be on the reviewing stand. "Damn! I haven't any gloves or a hat," she cried out.

"Neither do we," chimed in Peggy and Tina.

"Did you sweet young things think a medal presentation was going to be informal?" questioned Grandma Jackson, blue eyes twinkling over her glass of gin.

"I guess that means a quick trip to town," suggested Tommy's dad. Before his words hit the salt air, the ladies were on their way to the car. Grabbing the martini pitcher and hurrying to catch up, he called out, "Anyone for a toddy on the road?"

"Dress right, dress." This command shouted by the sergeant major ordered fifteen hundred men to raise their left arm parallel to the ground and turn their heads to the right. His next command "Cover" instructed the men to align themselves in straight lines, left and right, fore and aft. Satisfied with the results, he ordered "Front" followed by "Parade Rest." Lt. Col Wren was satisfied that the assembled group would pass muster and ordered the troops "At Ease" as they awaited the general's party to take their place on the reviewing stand.

When the general's adjutant bellowed the word "Group" it was echoed four times by company commandeers. The word "Attention" brought 1500 men to the position of attention with their heads up, chest out, heels together, feet at 45 degree angle and arms at their side with thumbs along the seams of their trousers.

"The following named officers will present themselves front and center; Captain Tommy Thompson and Captain Amos Jackson." The aviators stood at attention, not a hint of a smile on their faces, in front of the general as the adjutant read, "Citation to accompany the Awards of the Silver Star to Warrant Officer Amos Jackson and Warrant Officer Tommy Thompson, who distinguished themselves while participating in aerial flight as P-47 fighter pilots over Belgium on 12 November 1944. On this date, after they destroyed an enemy supply train,

Christmas Help

they engaged and destroyed four German Messerschmitt Bf-109's that were attacking a severely damaged American B-24 bomber. In spite of low ammunition, they elected to escort the heavily damaged aircraft back to its base in England. The heroism, valor and devotion to duty displayed by these officers reflects great credit upon themselves and the United State Army Air Corp."

The general stepped forward, pinned the medals on their chest and whispered, "Gentlemen, you two just don't know when to quit, do you?"

He stepped aside and the adjutant read, "Citation to accompany the award of the Distinguished Service Cross to Captain Tommy Thompson.

"Captain Tommy Thompson distinguished himself after being shot down on 15 February 1945. On this date, he assumed command of a truck convoy that was bringing a portable bridge to the east side of the Rhine River. This location was vital for the United States Third Army to enter Germany. His actions and leadership in organizing and holding a defensive position against a numerical superior enemy battalion were the key components in this successful operation. Captain Thompson's extraordinary heroism and unwavering willpower in the face of hostile forces reflect the highest credit upon himself and the United State Army Air Corp."

The general pinned the nation's second highest combat award on Tommy and, for a second, held the cross reverently with his finger tips. He looked Tommy straight in the eye and said "I'm honored to present this to you on behalf of a grateful nation."

The awards ceremony went flawlessly with only one exception. In that moment after the general finished pinning the medals on Tommy and Amos, Grandma Jackson hobbled forward and in a voice that could be heard across the parade ground, hollered, "Three cheers for these men and for all of you for bringing our nation to victory."

The general stepped up to her side and in his powerful voice roared, "Hip, hip…" Fifteen hundred men responded with an intensity similar to a symphony's crescendo, … with a "hurrah," vigorously three times.

The general took her arm and escorted her back to her seat. Bowing down close to her wrinkled face, he whispered, "If I didn't have a wife, I would pursue you."

She looked him straight in the eyes and said, "If you were twenty years older, I'd drag your skinny butt back to Texas."

Thirty six fighter aircraft in flights of four roared overhead, almost drowning out the base marching band playing the Army Air Corps song.

Peggy, Tina and Mary, with their wide brim hats shading their faces, had tears streaming down their cheeks. Their new white gloves were wet with the salty fluid. "Damn those two. If I would have known what risks he was taking, I would have boxed his ears," Peggy cried. 'Not once did he tell me what he experienced on those missions."

"Maybe one more swat with my switch would have taken some of that piss and vinegar out of Amos. I only wish his granddad could have been here to see all of this."

"*Sweetheart, I'm here thanks to Bartholomew,*" a familiar voice whispered ever so sweetly in her ear.

"*You know old man that we had to accept an extra lifetime or two of kicking tumbleweed to get you here,*" Bartholomew reminded him.

"*It'll be worth every damn minute,*" Granddad said as he was transported to his assigned area in west Texas.

Ten days later, the Japanese signed the terms of surrender that they declined after the Potsdam conference. And the day after that momentous event, an officers' call was held in the base theater.

"Gentlemen," the three star general began," I want you to know what a pleasure it has been serving with you all. Our victory has been bittersweet in that thousands of our comrades gave the ultimate sacrifice in defense of our country. They are the true heroes of this war. I have ordered that a letter be placed in your file confirming your individual efforts. There is in progress, even as I speak, a massive reduction in force. This means that most officers with reserve commissions will be released from active duty in the next ninety days. You have the presidents and the nation's undying gratitude for your service."

Second lieutenant Ogelsby took the general's place at the microphone and nervously gave instructions. "You will be scheduled for a separation briefing, alphabetically by rank, starting this afternoon. A determination of the number of points you have accrued will be made at that time. The schedule of appointments is posted on the bulletin boards. Thank you for your service to our country."

"Hey Lieutenant, what points are you talking about?"

"Gentlemen, The Advance Service Rating Score is a system to determine who gets sent home first. Points are awarded in five categories:

"You get one point for each month of service between 16 September 1940 and 12 May 1945.

"Add one point for each month of overseas service during the same time period.

"You heroes get 5 points for each medal awarded.

"Campaign stars on theater ribbons are worth 5 points to those who participated.

"And for you people that managed to screw your way to fatherhood, you get 12 points for each kid under eighteen. Being a lover rather than a fighter pays off.

"Add these up and 85 is the magic number for release from the service."

Some smart ass prophet grabbed the microphone as the stage was cleared. To that room full of surprised and confused officers, he offered, "Don't give up your commissions, gentlemen. They will always need Christmas help when our country bleeds again."

"Is that the regular officer corps' perception of the reserve officers? Christmas help?" a confused Amos uttered.

Shaking his head in disbelief at this unexpected turn of events, Tommy ventured, "Maybe not all the officers with regular commissions feel that way, but it appears the War Department looks on us reserves as part time killers." He put his arm on his wingman's shoulder and said, "Time to go to the house and share the news."

The atmosphere at the beach house ranged from confused to joyous. Tommy and Amos had been leaning toward a career in the military. After the first round of martinis, the impromptu party took on a serious turn. "Well partner, it looks like we are going to join the ranks of millions of unemployed ex-service men. Most of them, like you and me, never had a job before the army took us in. You and I have enough points to get out but even if we wanted to stay in, it isn't going to happen. To me and Tina with our sixteen oil wells, we'll always have grits on the table. But damn it, flying that P-80 has me cursed with the desire to fly faster and higher. Maybe I'll be able to buy one from the army surplus."

"Not with my dollars, Amos. I have other plans. If you want to tag along, I hear the big oil boys are going to Wyoming and that's where I'm headed with my purse full of nickels," chimed in Tina.

"What do you mean "If I want to tag along?" Whatever we decide, that's what we are going to do. Since I don't have the foggiest plan for the future, I'll go with yours. I've never thought about living on the Rocky Mountains, but if you promise not to put your cold feet on my back this winter, I'll go with you."

With her hands behind her back and her fingers crossed, a soft "I promise," passed Tina's lips. Mary and Peggy had a difficult time choking back a laugh.

Tommy placed a handful of medals on the kitchen table that he had retrieved from his dresser drawer. They were reminders of his thrills during his short lived military life. They also reminded him that they represented yesterdays. A time that was gone forever. He knew what they represented, but would a prospective employer place any value on them? Probably not…well, maybe only one.

"Tommy, how about joining me at Thompson Industry? The company's expanding and I could use some help. You've shown, according to all those awards and decorations, an ability to organize and lead. There's going to be some very large problems facing the nation as businesses change from a war to peace time economy. And on a smaller scale, Thompson Industries will share them. Besides, it's time you learned the business and I'd be proud to have you on board," piped in the company president of Thompson Industries.

The prospect of working for his dad didn't move his enthusiasm needle over the halfway mark, but there had to be a way to say 'maybe' without restarting the father son feud.

"Dad, I think I want to go to college." The smile on his father's face vanished.

"How are you going to manage that and provide for your wife?"

"There must be some assets I can sell from Aunt Molly's estate to finance part of the expense and start a home for Peggy and me. I heard there's talk of a G.I. Bill that may pay for the rest. Maybe you could use me part time."

The prospect of his son inching towards a position with his company and moving back home lifted his spirits. "There'll always be room for you part time or full time…and Peggy too. Since she's in that school of business, a little practical experience might prove to be helpful.

"That sounds like a great opportunity to me," Peggy quickly answered. "To be included as an intern in your business will make all the courses I'm taking take on a new meaning."

"Seems like everybody has a plan except John and Mary."

John had been hoping for the opportunity to approach the senior Thompson with a plan that Mary and he had been discussing for the last three days. "Mary, should I ask him?"

"Hell, all he can do is say no. Give it a try John. This is not the time to be bashful."

"This may not be the time or place, but we do have a plan that might be of interest to you. Mary and I want to get out of the North country. Our bones can't take the cold anymore, especially my legs. We kind of like this neck of the woods. Its warm and sometimes hot but we can get used to that."

"So you like the weather…doesn't sound like much of a plan to me," Mr. Thompson said, his eyes sparkling over his glass of scotch."

"We're hoping that when you send your business guests down here, we could be your representatives on site. We would pay you rent for the use of the guest house. We plan to set up a fishing boat business on the side. You have a nice dock and boat house that seems ideal for such a business. This is just a rough idea of our plans. If you're interested, we can get together and flesh out the details," John said rapidly without taking a breath.

"John your timing is perfect. Having family down here to protect my interests takes a load of worry off my mind. Your idea for a fishing boat business sounds interesting. I wonder if any of the locals will share their knowledge of these waters? This shoreline looks pretty tricky to me. Hell, when I went swimming the other day, I waded out over a fifty yards and the water was only up to my knees."

"Flying over the bay, I noticed at least three sunken boats. I'm sure there are other hazards that I missed," piped in Amos.

"I think with a little help and a little time common sense, I can figure these problems out," John asserted. "We're talking fishing here, not quantum physics."

"I invited Dr. Dan Bowers and his wife Ann over for dinner and drinks this evening. Perhaps he can recommend someone that might have the right background," Tommy offered.

During dinner, John kept staring at Dr. Dan, and just as the lime pie was being served, he jumped up, pointed at him and shouted, "You're the one, sure as hell you're the one!"

Not knowing if a fight was about to break out, Bowers slid his chair back, clenched his fists and said, "I'm the one what?"

"You're the one who operated on me in France during the first war," John confidently proclaimed.

"I'm sorry, I don't remember you…there were so many."

"I was the one who grabbed you by the throat and threatened to kill you if you amputated my legs."

"Well, I'll be damned. Now I remember. It took three orderlies to hold you down and put you under. I should have gotten the Purple Heart for that bruise you left on my neck. As I recall, you motivated me to reconsider my first opinion that your mangled legs had to go. Then I figured you had enough determination to make it through a long and painful recovery period. I did my best to save your legs. Obviously my best was good enough. I never saw you after the operation."

"Doc, I can dance like Fred Astaire thanks to you. You have my neverending appreciation," John said as he made his way to the doctor and gave him a hug that surprised both wives.

"One can never guess what those old leathernecks are going to do next," sighed Mary.

"Oh, I can not only guess but can predict with a high degree of certainty they will go drink and toast each other until they drop. And then I get to drive home again," Ann Bowers said wearily.

"We have extra rooms here, so why not stay here tonight?" suggested Peggy. There is also some fine wine that we girls can liberate for our gab fest. I think the boys are in a war story mood and I've had my fill of that."

"Wait until you've heard those stories twenty times, then you'll really have your fill of them," Mary injected as she grabbed two bottles of imported cabernet sauvignon.

"There is nothing more tasteless then after dinner reminiscing of removing shattered arms and limbs," Ann Bowers remarked, as she gathered the shrimp dip and chips.

"Being a newcomer to the veterans' ladies auxiliary gab fests, I promise to gossip only about that horny colonel with the wandering hands," Tina added with a devilish smile.

"Really Tina, I thought all colonels thought they were God's gift to officers' wives. I remember that after one of the first war's victory balls this obnoxious old bird trying his luck out on me. Dan didn't take kindly and flattened him right there on the dance floor. That event hastened our departure from the corps."

All the ladies were in agreement that these tales were best told away from their husbands. So out to the porch, swinging on the gliders, sipping a sweet white wine, the wives' war stories unfolded before the first shot of the first war was told…

Chapter 33

"Keep in touch, Amos. Keep that peter heater that Mary knitted handy. You're going to need it on those mountain tops. Stay warm, old buddy."

"You too, partner. I'll never forget you. With any luck we'll join together as we did cruising in the blue. Remember, check six."

Peggy and Tina smiled and gave each other a hug then climbed into their cars, tears rolling down their cheeks. The cars rolled down state highway 98 following each other until the highway split. One segment continued west and the other headed north. Peggy and Tina waved at each other until they were out of sight.

"Don't look so sad, Tommy. We'll meet them again... someday...I hope."

Shaking off the same empty feeling he had when his mother died, "You're right, sweetheart. I'll try to make sure that meeting happens."

"Really Tommy, you haven't had much luck in making things turn out the way you want them."

"What are you talking about?"

"Like your plans to stay in the air corps. You just knew that when you won that DSC …"

"I didn't win any medal, I earned each and every one of them."

"Let me finish, please."

"Go right ahead," Tommy said through tight lips.

"When you earned that DSC, you just knew that you would be offered a regular commission and get to fly your precious jet airplanes. Well that didn't happen, did it?"

"No, it didn't. Where are you going with this tirade?"

"Tirade…I'll give you tirade," as she whacked his arm.

"Damn it. Knock it off. Do you want me to lose control of the car?"

"Well you've lost control of everything else."

Tommy checked the rearview mirror, saw no one behind him, and slammed on the brakes. Peggy put her hands on the dashboard and kept herself from hitting the windshield. Tommy eased the car off the road and turned to Peggy.

"What in the hell is wrong with you?"

"Not once did you ask me what I wanted to do…or where I wanted to live. It's been all about you."

"Okay, what do want to do and where do you want to live?"

Christmas Help

"I want to finish my two years at the university and live in a nice apartment close to the campus. That's what I want. I'm not cut out to be a farmer's wife."

"And I'm not cut out to be a farmer. But I will if I have to. I don't have the money to rent an apartment. Our choices are, we live with my dad, we live with your parents, you live in the dorm and I live out at the farm or we live at the farm. You have the next fifteen hundred miles during which you can make up your mind." Peggy started to cry as Tommy pushed hard on the accelerator to get back on the highway. The semi-trailer's horn almost deafened them as the truck driver expertly avoided the collision. Tommy eased back on to the highway's shoulder, his hands and knees shaking uncontrollably.

I thought my job would be easier when no one's shooting at him, but it appears that whether it's peace or war, an angel has to keep his head on a swivel in order to ward off danger.

Tommy grabbed Peggy and held her close for several minutes. When her sobbing stopped and his body quit shaking, they both started to say, "I'm sorry" but a kiss interrupted the apology.

"Tommy, you know I love you, but right now I don't like you," the frown on her face gave emphasis to her words. Tommy gripped the steering wheel tightly and drove on with out a response.

Four long days on the road and four nights in the cheapest motels didn't solve the problem that had surfaced on the first day. Tommy kept pitching his remembrances of the farm in glowing terms but Peggy conceded nothing. On the outskirts of Madison, Tommy stopped the car and said, "Decision time. Where do you want me to go?"

Without looking at him, her arms folded across her chest, she said, "Farm."

Driving up the dirt road leading to the house Peggy blurted out,"You don't expect me to milk all those cows, do you?"

"I don't know who those cows belong to, but they sure as hell aren't mine."

They arrived at the house Tommy's aunt had left him in her will. They thought they were ready to start life in the civilian world, ten miles north of Madison, Wisconsin. What they found was a house trashed by the renters who were obviously more than unhappy that they had been forced to leave.

"So this is that cute, spick and span home your aunt lived in. Unbelievable."

"Damn, damn, damn," Tommy muttered as he kicked aside a basket of rotting garbage blocking the kitchen entrance. The basket tumbled and added to the mess under the kitchen sink. A fat mouse scurried across the linoleum and escaped through the kitchen door. Both Peggy and Tommy jumped with alarm and threw their arms around each other. They laughed then pushed each other away. Nervously they searched for any other unwanted critters.

"Looks like they kept their dogs in this room," Peggy said, holding her nose and reluctantly venturing towards the downstairs bathroom. "They didn't even flush the toilet. At least they used the pot."

"Hello there…Anybody home?"

"Come on in, but watch your step."

"I'm Steve Jensen and this is my wife Beverly. We're your neighbors on the farm to your west. Looks like your tenants played hell with this place."

"I'm Tommy Thompson and this is my wife Peggy. Pleasure to meet you…forgive the mess…we just got here."

"My wife and I were here about two hours ago hoping to welcome you home. We couldn't believe our eyes when we ventured in through the open door. We went back home and called our church welcoming committee. They said they would be here shortly with as many volunteers as they could round up on this Sunday morning. Could we go outside and talk…my eyes are starting to burn."

Cars and pickup trucks were kicking up dust as they approached the house. Steve greeted each one, introduced them to the Thompsons and gave instructions on what they were to work on or clean up.

"You three men go upstairs with Tommy and either haul those broken bedroom furniture pieces down or throw them out the windows. I think two of you can get those crates and chairs out of the living room and on to our burn pile. I'll need help with that mess in the basement.

"Ladies, I wouldn't dare tell you how to cleanup that kitchen, but I'm sure you can get these strapping teenage boys to assist you. Come on guys…get those frowns off your faces. That kitchen isn't that big."

"Now you young ones start a fire in that clearing. Gather the trash and stay upwind from the smoke. Did I mention don't get burned?"

"No sir, you didn't."

"Well don't."

"Rollie, Do you need any help getting the water well pump operating?"

"Have I ever needed help with machinery, Steve?"

"Not that I can remember."

"Well then you get on with your rat killing and let me be."

A fire was started in the clearing and the kids kept the blaze going for hours. Watchful eyes kept tabs on the little ones. It took an occasional sharp word from an adult to keep the fire brigade in line. A lower lip would eke out, someone's feelings were bruised, but discipline was maintained.

A gaggle of teen age boys were sent to scrub windows and floors. They displayed little enthusiasm for this chore but with their mothers overseeing their efforts, the task was completed flawlessly.

"My mom uses vinegar and water to clean windows."

"It's going to take a couple of gallons to make these transparent," offered a red headed beanpole.

"Vinegar isn't going to clean the mess on the floor… looks like good old smelly Lysol is needed. Open the windows for cryin' out loud. You want to suffocate us?"

"Hey Joey, you missed that dog crap in the corner."

"Yes'm, I see it, I'm just trying to get a breath of fresh air."

"Don't dilly dally…clean it up."

"Yes'm."

Some of the older men cut weeds that had taken over the garden and flower beds.

"I can't believe these radishes and cucumbers have survived. Look at those pumpkins. Doggone near blue ribbon winners. Hell this may be the future of farming. Just throw the seeds at the ground, forget them and then harvest them at your leisure." They had a good laugh at this suggestion as they continued to hoe the weeds into oblivion.

Four hours later, two pickup trucks arrived carrying three picnic tables and baskets of food. As the sun settled, a call to dinner was answered by a tired crowd of volunteers. Tommy was asked to say the blessing.

"Lord, thank you for neighbors that helped a stranger in need. And to my new neighbors and friends, I say thank you. Our home will always be open to all of you. Peggy and I are forever in your debt. Amen."

"Captain you have that all wrong. We're in your debt not only for your service to our country but mostly for your efforts as a kid delivering medicine and food to our parents and grandparents. You made their lives a little bit easier and at times you wouldn't take a nickel for your efforts." Steve ran his fingers through his graying hair and concluded, "Welcome home neighbor."

Tommy and Peggy shook every hand as the volunteers departed. Steve and Beverly were the last to climb into their truck. "Tommy, I don't know how much you know about farming…"

"I know nothing, Steve."

"I was going to remind you that you better get going on mowing your hay fields. There's rain in the seven day forecast and you might lose the crop."

"Is there anyone in that group that helped me, that needs any or all of it? I don't have any way of cutting it or using it. I hate to see it go to waste."

"There's two families that really can use it but won't be able to pay you the going rate."

"Tell them it's theirs if they cut it and haul it off."

"Tommy, you're giving up a sizable chunk of money…do you really want to do that?"

"They helped me, and this is my way of paying them back."

Reaching through the open window, he grabbed Tommy's hand and said, "They'll be here tomorrow morning, bright and early. You're going to be a hell of a neighbor."

"By the way Steve, do you know who owns those cows?"

"Those would be free loading Barnaby's. I've chased his herd off my property a couple times. He thinks the world owes him a living. I've offered to lease him some acreage at a reasonable rate, but he wants it free."

"Well I'll talk to him and see what kind of deal we can make."

"Don't waste your time Tommy. I'll have them cows back on his property early tomorrow morning."

"Thanks Steve."

Peggy looked at her husband, patted him on his fanny and remarked, "Before you give away the rest of the farm, let's see if we can find something to sleep on." He picked her up and started to carry her across the threshold.

"Stop and take those dirty boots off. That kitchen floor is spotless and that's the way it's going to stay."

"Yes, precious."

The never ending dream seemed so real to Tommy. He was covered in dirt and the bodies of the two British and one German infantry men. The sound of the tanks made his eardrums ache. His arms were flailing and he called out for Bart.

"Tommy, are you all right? You sure have made a tangled mess of the covers and quilt. And who is Bart?"

"I don't know Peggy, I guess he was part of my dream. Where is that roar coming from? Did the war start again? Are those tanks using our driveway?"

Peggy was up looking out the window when a kid in a baseball cap waved to her from the tractor pulling a mower. "Tommy, it's just 6:30 and there are three more tractors coming down the road."

Jumping up from the mattress on the floor, he half yelled, "Better put some coffee on and I'll run and get some eggs and bacon for them when they're ready." He was pulling up his pants when he heard, a woman yell "Anybody home?"

He was greeted at the bottom of the stairs by Steve's wife, who had a basket full of groceries. "Thought I'd save you a trip to town. The Simmons' boys, that's who'll be mowing your hay as soon as the dew burns off. Their Mother Susie sent over a smoked ham and a couple dozen eggs to get you started. The vegetables are from my garden. We had a bountiful harvest this year and I've canned enough for two winters. Anyway, I got to get going to my job at the university."

"You work there?"

"In admissions," she replied, hurrying out the door.

"That's where I'll be going this morning, to see if the university will accept me."

Beverly halted her departure. "Be there at 10 o'clock and ask for me. By the way, Steve moved those cows back to Barnaby's farm. He's madder than a wet hen. Probably be over to see you soon…that should be fun. See ya."

* * *

"That was a quick trip. Did they accept you?"

Whirling Peggy around the kitchen in his stocking feet, "They admitted me as a junior! Beverly gave me two years credit for my military experience. My major is in Military Science and I'll minor in Engineering. I hope she didn't break any rules and get herself in trouble on my behalf. I'm so happy I want to celebrate."

"Well come with me and we'll celebrate by pulling weeds out of the garden. Those Simmons boys took a half hour break for lunch and said they would have it all cut by sundown. Tomorrow they'll be back to rake it and if the weather holds, they will have it bailed by the weekend."

"Aren't they a little young to be doing all this?"

"That's the question I asked them. They laughed and said they been running the farm ever since their daddy was drafted. He sent all but two dollars of his private's pay home each month but that didn't stretch very far. Since he got discharged, he's been working in town at a gas station to pay off some loans. He lost a hand at Anzio and is struggling to keep his head above water. The boys say he is a great farmer."

"I'd like to meet him."

"You will tonight when he inspects the boys' work. Now put a little back into that hoeing or we'll never get done."

A loud "Hey you," interrupted their work. They turned as a large overweight man in bib overalls ambled towards them. He carried a large stick and his red face indicated he was either angry or out of breath. "Who do you think you are running my cattle off like that?"

"I'm Tommy Thompson and this is my wife Peggy." He stepped between Peggy and this intruder, not taking his eyes off the stick. "You must be Barnaby."

He started to yell, "That I am…you had no right to…"

"Hold it right there Mr. Barnaby. Those cows were on my property illegally. Either get a civil tongue in your mouth or get off my land."

"You shinny little shit, you can't make me," he shouted, moving forward.

Tommy knocked the stick out of his hand with his hoe and put the handle four inches into Barnaby's fat stomach and through clenched teeth hissed, "Get."

"This isn't over," he mumbled slowly, walking away.

That evening Tommy's body was half under the hood of one of his clunkers in the barn, a 1936 Ford four door convertible. The top was so fragile Tommy was afraid to touch it. From out of the shadows, a crisp voice announced, "Captain, I'm Simmons." The greeting startled him and he bumped his head as he came out of the engine compartment.

"Please call me Tommy," he said as he rubbed the back of his head and extended his other hand. An artificial hand awkwardly met his.

"I want to tell you that I intend to pay you for that hay, Captain."

"Like hell you will. I'm repaying, as best I can, the clean up work that you and the Lutheran church group did for me and my wife. So I don't want to hear another word about the damn hay…except that your sons are doing one hell of a job.'

"Captain, I don't want charity."

Ignoring Simmons remark, Tommy asked, "Are you a mechanic?"

"Yes sir."

"Well tell me, what am I doing wrong? I can't keep the motor running more than a few seconds at a time."

"Move over and let me take a look…here's the problem. The sediment bowl is full of crap. How old is that gas?"

"Probably three years if it's a day."

"Drain the tank…clean out the bowl…put some fresh fuel in it and if it doesn't run, I'll kiss your ass."

"You have a way with words, Simmons. Come inside and have a cup of coffee."

"A quick cup and then I'll be on my way, Captain."

Peggy set three cups of coffee and a plate of hot cinnamon rolls on the table. "Damn, we haven't had cinnamon rolls over at the house in a coon's age…they taste delicious. Thank you, ma'am."

"Since we're neighbors, cut out the ma'am and Captain. I'm Peggy and this is Tommy. What's your first name Mr. Simmons?"

"People around here call me Rollie. Only my mother gets to calls me Roland."

Tony Skur

"Well Rollie, your sons tell us you're a great farmer."

"Damn right, I am. Been farming since I finished the seventh grade. Even took night classes in agriculture at the university till the government up and drafted my ass. Sorry Peggy for that slip of my tongue. I couldn't believe they needed me more than my family did. Here I was, thirty five years old with a wife and three sons and they ship my behind off to war. And that lousy twenty one dollars a month sure made life tough on the family. My sons, God bless them, kept the farm running and the bank let me go in debt deep enough so that they own more of the land than I do. But by God, I ain't going to give up," slamming his metal hand on the table causing another dent in already distressed table top.

Startled, Peggy looked at Tommy and nodded her head. "Rollie," Tommy started, "Peggy and I have a problem and we hope you can solve it."

"If it's a loan you need, I ain't got two pennies to rub together."

"No, our problem is that we don't know beans about farming and we have two hundred acres of land out there adjacent to yours."

"And it's mighty good farm land, Tommy," Rollie said with a mouth full of cinnamon roll.

"I was thinking if you let your cows graze on half of my acreage and fertilize it, I could plant hay on the other half. Then the year after that I would switch them around…"

Rollie burst out laughing, almost choking on the sip of coffee he had just put to his lips. "You must have grown up in the city, Tommy. Cows don't fertilize, they just crap."

Blushing Tommy replied, "I told you I didn't know beans about farming. Do you have the time and the inclination to manage and work the land? I believe a profit could be made…"

Sitting up straight on the wooden kitchen chair, his coffee cup clanged when he hit it with his artificial hand. "I'll tell you right now that I can make a profit off your land without breaking a sweat. What kind of arrangement do you have in mind?"

Tommy leaned back and spoke the words that Peggy and him had agreed on. "You make all the decisions to get this farm up and running, leaving one acre around the house for Peggy and me to try to garden. Tell me where you intend to buy the necessary seed and equipment and I'll set up an account. Peggy's a lot better with taking care of money and bills and she will take on this chore."

"We have the same money management philosophy at our house. My wife Susie can squeeze that buffalo nickel until it shits and then sell the manure to city folk. Again excuse my French, Peggy. What percentage of profits do you want?"

"We would want 20 percent."

Scratching his head, Rollie answered, "Are you two nuts? Fifty fifty is the going rate."

"You'll be doing all the work and I hope teaching us. I don't know how much time is involved with doing our university schedule, but getting our degrees is our priority. Twenty percent is what we want. So Rollie, is this a good deal for both of us or not?"

A smile spread across his grease streaked face. "It's a great deal for me, and if twenty percent will keep you two happy then I'm tickled shitless… excuse my French Peggy…with the deal. Do you want me to sign some papers?"

"I think a hand shake should do it…you have that and my word."

Rollie stood to shake Tommy's hand. "Good enough, neighbor. You're an officer and a gentleman and I hear tell that an officer's word is his bond. I'll be going and let the family know what we've agreed to and make plans for my sons' work schedule."

Handing Rollie a paper sack full of warm rolls, "For the boys and Susie," Peggy said. "See your sons tomorrow morning."

Before Rollie's sons arrived, the sheriff knocked at the kitchen door. "Mrs. Thompson, I'm Sherriff Swenson I'm here to…"

"You're the officer that didn't give Tommy a ticket for speeding the night he came home from the war. And then you escorted us to the Concourse Hotel. You're the first and only police officer I've kissed."

Turning a plum red, he admitted he remembered a

beautiful young woman and a decorated pilot. "I'm here to speak to your husband. Is he available?"

"He's out back mending a fence…are you here because of that run in with Mr. Barnaby?"

"Yes… he filed a complaint against your husband alleging he attacked him without provocation."

"All Tommy did after Barnaby verbally abused him and moved forward with that stick is defend me and put the hoe handle in his belly. I see Tommy coming this way. How about some breakfast?"

"I hate to bother you, but Barnaby had me up and out here before I had a cup of coffee. Thank you, I will."

Slipping his boots off, Tommy looked at the law man dipping his toast into his sunny side up trio of eggs. "I remember you, sheriff. Pour me a cup, honey," he remarked as he sat down at the table.

"Wish I could have been here before Barnaby showed up. He's the biggest pain in the ass in the county. I've fielded more complaints on him and his damn herd of cows than protests on the drunken brawls over at the Body Exchange Bar."

"I'm truly sorry that we couldn't have settled this peacefully." Tommy lamented. "Now what?"

"Now nothing. I'll tell him I've laid the law down to you…and I'll tell him to quit trespassing. If that doesn't work, then I guess I'll just have to shoot him. Just joking. May I have a couple more eggs and toast?"

Chapter 34

The gentle breeze moved the tassel on Tommy's cap ever so slightly and the movement brought his attention back to the commencement speaker.

"This graduating class of 1947 has the potential and I believe the opportunity to cure the ills of this great nation of ours. It will be up to you to…"

I don't know where this politician' speech is headed, but in the last twenty minutes he has predicted our class will save the world and the university from every evil ranging from corn aphids to communism. Tommy's eyes wandered from the politician to the flag fluttering behind him.

"You have had the privilege to attend this great university and learn valuable information from scholars who…"

Glancing to his left, his wife's smile indicated her mind was focused on something other than the speech. Peggy's looking beautiful in her cap and gown. She has a glow about her that I expect comes from finishing her finals. Her sheep skin will have magna cum laude emblazoned on it.

"Those of you who have earned your degree with magna cum laude have a special responsibility to…"

Magna cum laude my ass, Peggy thought. Those old fogy's didn't praise me. They just kept reminding me how lucky I was to be included in an all male discipline. Well I showed them. All it took was eight hours of studying after every class and putting up with countless put downs by my so called male peers. The only thing equal was the opportunity.

"So as you go forward carrying the banner of this great university, remember…"

Scratching his head, Tommy reflected I'm perfectly happy with cum laude. Hell, that's a lie. I'm perfectly miserable sitting here growing roots. The last two years haven't exactly flown by…maybe that's the problem. I want back in the air. His ears picked up the sound before the smart remarks came over the loud speakers.

"Well it appears that the air corps is up bright and early. Ladies, I hope you'll raise your sons to be more courteous than those cowboys flying overhead wasting our tax dollars and disturbing this assembly. As I was saying before I was so rudely interrupted…"

That's what I want…I want the freedom of flight. But that's not going to happen. I'll be stuck working the farm and working for Dad. I can't think of two more boring prospects for employment. Peggy, on the other hand, loves the responsibilities that Dad has given her and keeps asking for more. She's still not keen on being at the farm, but at times seems to enjoy the success we have made of it.

"If you remember any of the lessons you learned during the last four years, I hope it's...

What I really learned surprised me, Peggy thought. At first I thought living out on the farm was a big mistake. But with Rollie managing and his sons working the land, Tommy and I were able to concentrate on our studies. There wasn't the hustle and bustle of city life, but there was time for our farming community of friends. Actually life has been grand.

"Go forward, try not to repeat your mistakes. Remember who you are and what you are and the difference between the two."

Well he got that part right. I know the difference but unfortunately my father doesn't. Dad has sensed my reluctance but hasn't pushed me into accepting the leadership of the company. I worked hard at getting this degree and feel a little proud of myself for hanging in there. But with the degree comes decision time…damn, damn, damn.

"So in conclusion, I offer this graduating class my heartfelt congratulations and sincere wish for successful careers."

"Tommy, stand up," Peggy whispered as she nudged him. "Time to gather in the fruits of our labors."

Moving with the group as they stepped forward to receive their undergraduate degrees, Peggy's smile reflected the pride she felt in completing her grueling schedule. Tommy's stoic look was that of a condemned prisoner. He did manage a thin smile as he shook the senator's hand. He closed the short distance from Peggy, grabbed her hand, and twirled her to him with just enough force that their tassels entwined. He kissed her lips hidden between the gold strands hanging from their caps and was rewarded with the quickest dart of her tongue. "Let's go home," both said with a look that promised a graduation present to remember.

Unfortunately, at home there was a gathering of friends and neighbors on this Sunday in May of 1947. Some were sitting on folded chairs around card tables. Others had lawn chair strategically placed under a stand of oak trees. While others were clustered around a picnic table loaded with refreshments. They were bent on celebrating the young couple's scholastic achievement and recalling their involvement with the farming community

"Looks like we got here just in time. In fact, the party is well on the way," Peggy noted. "Our neighbors have prepared a small mountain of food. They know their hard working husbands are not shy about helping themselves to second and third helpings."

"I can smell those bratwurst, summer sausage, knockwursts and baked chicken. That should put a dent in their appetites. I bet that baked ham dominating the center of the table came from the Simmons," Tommy suggested. This feast was flanked by three types of potato salad, coleslaw and baskets of homemade wheat and rye bread all lined up on a picnic table covered with a blue checkered cloth.

"My relish dishes are almost hidden among the heaps of freshly churned butter. Good God, there's enough mayonnaise to spread evenly across half the state," Peggy said.

"And boy oh boy, that side table has at least a dozen pies," Tommy said, licking his lips. "Apple pies, lemon meringue pies, banana cream pies, peach pies…even one of Beverly's blue ribbon rhubarb pies. I may regret it tomorrow, but I'm going to try a small slice of each."

Peggy's mom and dad provided an enormous bowl of tartar de bough and a mound of sliced onions. Tommy's dad brought a keg of beer, a half dozen bottles of whiskey and enough soft drinks to keep the young ones away from the beer…he hoped.

"I think we better watch those Simmons' boys. They seem to be getting their share of beer by being courteous and asking the adults if they could refill their glasses for them. That route they traverse from the keg back to the tables is shielded by a grape arbor. I bet this is where an inch or two of that golden brew mysteriously disappears. Hell, they're almost seventeen. And their daddy's driving." Tommy and Peggy left them to their game.

Later Rollie cornered Tommy between the tractor and the barn. He nervously clanked his metal hand against the John Deere tractor's green fender. His good hand had Tommy by the back of his neck holding him in place. His face, inches from Tommy's, was almost in tears and his breath held a hint of rye whiskey. "Thank you Captain for all you've given me and my family."

"All I've given you is a hell of lot of back breaking work, Rollie."

"Captain, you've given me the opportunity to get out of debt and if the good Lord's willing, when this year's crop is in the silo, we'll put a few dollars in the saving's account. Since you finished your schooling, I suspect you'll want to be more involved with running the farm. I'll back away from the decision making. I think you and your lady have the hang of it."

"Rollie, let's not change anything until this fall. I'm trying to figure out what it is I want to do with my life."

"Damn, I would give anything for that option. But at the same time overseeing your farm a while longer might give me a money cushion to fall back on." Reaching into his overall pockets with his metal hand, he pulled out a bundle of letters. Releasing Tommy from his powerful grip, he jerked out his red bandana, wiped his eyes and blew his nose with a ferocity that sent the chickens scurrying across the yard.

"My youngest picked up your mail the last day of school, stuck it in his school bag and promptly forgot about it. If that half eaten apple hadn't started to stink, your mail would have been in there until school started. That whack his momma gave him will improve his memory. Sorry about that, Captain."

Glancing at the stack of mail, Tommy said, "Hell Rollie, they look like bills…don't worry about it," he said shoving the mail in his back pocket. "How about a beer?"

"Let me offer my congratulations to Peggy then I'll meet you at the keg."

The last inebriated guest, the oldest and most courteous Simmons boy Joey, was hauled off by his ear, struggling to keep up with his mother. Tommy knew better than to intercede on the teenager's behalf and busied himself picking up the few cups and plates left on the tables. The packed Simmons' car's noise level faded as it turned towards home. The quiet darkness was interrupted by Peggy's call, "We can finish up tomorrow.

Tommy led Peggy to their bedroom. Their gentle kisses became more furious as they removed each others' clothes. Their naked bodies basked in the moonlight streaming in through the open window.

The promised graduation gift to each other was delivered with loving passion.

Sitting at the breakfast table, picking at the party's left over chicken and apple pie ,they were sorting out the bills from the stack of mail, Peggy slid one over to Tommy and murmured, "This one looks official. It's registered. Did you sign for it?"

"No. I bet Rollie's youngest did. It's probably from the bank. Nope, it's from the Defense Department," he said, louder than he intended. Ripping open the envelope, he sang, "I'll be damned. I'm being called to active duty with the Army Air Force as a pilot with the rank of captain. I'm to report in at Scott Field in Illinois on the fifteenth of June and await a follow on assignment." The big grin on his face disappeared when he looked at Peggy… tears ran down her cheeks. "Hey, don't cry… this will be a fun thing and probably won't last forever."

"Fun for you, but I'm pregnant. I was going to tell you later tonight," she blubbered.

Tommy's chair fell back as he jumped to his feet. "You're what?"

Waving her hands in front of her stomach she cried, "Pregnant…you know… with child. I didn't want to tell you when I first found out, because you've been in such a rotten mood. Everything out of your mouth was damn house, damn car, damn farm. I certainly didn't want to hear damn kid." She threw herself at him, beating him on his chest. Her sobbing was not exactly hysterically but intense enough to scare the hell out of Tommy.

"Please honey," he whispered, his face buried in her hair. "Please stop crying." Gently rubbing her shoulders and with a smile that lit up the room, he proclaimed, " I'm so happy and proud. I'm going to be a father. But with all that time you spent studying, how did you manage to get pregnant?"

"You big dummy," she cried, "you should have taken a biology course instead of advanced calculus."

Chapter 35

The oscillating fan barely kept the sweat off Tommy's face as he waited in line to process back into the military. He overheard the frazzled clerk explain five times that he didn't know why all you gentlemen were recalled. "My guess is when they released everyone at the end of the war, the Army Air Corp personnel dropped from two point five million troops to 304,000. A couple, two, three months ago, the generals got worried. Then President Truman got worried and here you are representing your neighbors again."

"I read that there's only 30,000 aircraft left out of the 79,000 we had at the end of the war," interjected a lanky hayseed looking man.

Looking up from his stack of papers, the sergeant continued, "Let me guess, you're the double ace, right?"

"Yup, that's me."

"Well sir, you'll be less than happy to hear that we only have 177 bases left from our high of 783 to park them on."

"Hell sergeant, that's only 21 more bases than we had when the war started."

"It's like my daddy used to say sir, 'Chicken one day, feathers the next.' Next in line please."

"Captain Thompson, if you will step over to that line by the major's office, he has some news for you. Don't look so worried captain, his bark isn't as bad as his bite."

"Thank you for those words of comfort, Sergeant."

Fifteen minutes later, the major invited him in and gave him an option, "Thompson, in September the Army Air Corp will become a separate service. Because of your combat record, a panel of generals have selected you, if you're willing, to be in the initial cadre of the United States Air Force. If you decide that you want no part of the new service, then the Army Air Corp would be delighted to have you on board."

"Major, which service will end up with the fighter aircraft?"

"The Air Force gets them all and most of the heavies."

"Then you have a volunteer, sir. Where do I sign?"

"Right here on this line. You'll be permanent party here at Scott Field until September…then I suspect there will be an overseas assignment for you. Have you checked in at the bachelor officers' quarters?"

"Yes sir, I have."

"There are four P-51's down on the flight line. Get fitted with some personal equipment and get some flying time in one those sweet machines."

Christmas Help

"Sir, I haven't flown a fifty one before."

"Damn it Captain, you got wings and according to your record you've got balls. There's a dash one at base ops. Take a look see at it before you crank it up. Get enough flying time in it so that you're comfortable. If you're so inclined, take one cross country but don't bend it. The clerk will cut you orders. And by the way, hang your uniform out where it will get a good airing. It smells like mothballs."

The NCO at base ops handed him the dash one, the Basic Flight Manual on the P-51, and asked, "Captain, have you flown a fifty one before?"

"No Sergeant, I haven't."

"Do you want some stay alive hints on how that baby handles?"

"Sure do, Sergeant. Is there any one around here that's flown the Mustang?"

"I had over a thousand hours in that jewel before they RIF'ed me. Buy me a cup of coffee, and I'll teach you how not to bust your ass, sir."

One hour later and ten rules of truism later, Tommy eased himself into the cockpit of this legendary fighter. He inhaled the aroma given up by the cramped compartment's interior. A combination of sweat, aviation gas and hydraulic fluid fumes lingered in the humid air. This is where I belong, he thought. Engine and flight instruments are placed in a perfect position. He practiced his cross check until there were no wasted seconds searching the panel for the indicator he wanted. The instruments came to life as the Packard-Merlin 1380 horse power engine's exhaust roared its willingness to become airborne.

On the active runway, Tommy eased the throttle forward. The engine's torque wanted to pull the aircraft to the left. Right rudder kept the nose spinner on the center line of the runway. His left turn out of traffic was interrupted by a flash of navy blue that was pulling streamers off the wing tips of the gull winged Corsair. His first reaction was to push in full throttle and pull his aircraft into a tail chase…then a recent truism flashed in his mind, don't pull heavy "Gs" with a full fuel load his sergeant instructor emphasized, this baby will swap ends and you'll be in a death spin. I think I owe that base ops sergeant another cup of java.

After two hours of stalls, slow flight and then some acrobatics, a sweat drenched Tommy brought the aircraft back to the field for some touch and go landings. The first ones were nothing to write home about. The skips and bounces forced a light laugh from Bartholomew.

Come on Tommy, you can do better than that…get the airspeed under control and put this critter where you want it, not the other way around.

On his fourth try, he found the correct attitude and airspeed and felt like he and the P-51 were one. The tires on his last landing squeaked, announcing a perfect three point touchdown. The smile on his face as he deplaned was silent testimony to his self confidence.

"Hot damn Captain, you got a feel for this mustang that most pilots don't find until they have a couple hundred hours in the bird. And I'm proud as punch you didn't take after that Corsair. We'd be picking your body parts out of that cornfield. Have a cigar on me," offered the envious RIF'd sergeant.

"Thanks, but I don't smoke...and by the by, I owe you another cup of Joe."

"Hell, Captain, all fighter pilots worth their salt smoke cigars...and I accept your offer for that cup of java."

"In that case, got a match for this born again fighter pilot?" He coughed as he inhaled and thought, *this doesn't taste half bad.*

Bartholomew was leaning against a limp wind sock pole thinking, *I better check that supply of luck. I think I hear the drums of war off in the distance and Tommy's got that gleam in his eye.*

The tower operator saw the blinding flash and wondered what happened to the wind sock pole.

Bartholomew found himself next to Grandpa Jackson as he kicked a tumbleweed across the highway. "Glad to see you young man, I can use some help."

Chapter 36

They were all waving their hats as he flew low over the farmhouse. He could see Peggy in the garden looking up, her hand shielding her eyes. It's been two months since he left her and he wasn't looking forward to telling her about his next assignment. The drive way to the house was clear of cars. He rechecked the landing gear handle down. Full flaps and power and a little bit of cross control allowed him to crab the aircraft straight down the road. He kicked his rudder at precisely the right half second and the P-51 touched down gently in a full stall. He closed the throttle and coasted up to the barn.

"You boys put a couple of pieces of firewood behind and in front of the wheels," he yelled to the Simmons brothers.

Peggy stood there with her hands on her hips. "I don't think you came here unannounced to give me a ride in your new toy."

"No, I came here to give you a big kiss…a kiss for both of you." With great care he started to pulled her towards him. She grabbed him and pulled him hard to her body. "I'm not going to break." Two months of longing for each other was almost satisfied in the embrace that brought whistles from the Simmons boys.

"Let me show the boys how to get up in the cockpit and a quick lesson on what not to touch. Shouldn't take but a minute."

Thirty minutes and a thousand questions later, he arrived in the kitchen as Peggy put a pan of cinnamon rolls in the oven. "Is it my turn now to ask a few questions… the most important one being, when do I join you at Scott Field?"

"Yesterday they gave me orders to go to an infantry platoon leadership school in Texas and then to a jump school in Georgia."

"What are you talking about? What in the hell is a jump school?"

"It's a course in parachuting out of airplanes…"

"Let me get this straight…after you crashed landed six P-47s they're going to teach you how to parachute out of a perfectly good airplane…then they just got you started in a brand new Air Force and they're sending you to an infantry school. Tommy what's this all about? And who the hell is they?"

"Honey, when I finish those schools, I'll be going to Korea."

"Just where in the hell is Korea?"

"A country almost next to Japan…I think the rolls are burning.'

"That's me that's burning," she screamed as she made a bee line for the oven. "Tommy, you're not telling me every thing…what's that roar?"

Tommy sprinted towards the aircraft just as the engine hit a smooth idle.

The oldest Simmons boy had a smile on his face that Tommy wanted to slap off but then he remembered answering all of his questions and should have figured out why the kid asked them. That airplane wasn't any more difficult to start then some of those big tractors that kid had been driving. The other boys were about to remove the logs holding the wheels in place as Tommy grabbed them by the shoulders and pulled them away.

The eldest boy saw Tommy and retarded the throttle to the cut off position. As Tommy put his head in the cockpit just as the cover snapped down over the master switch.

"I'm going into the Air force just as soon as I graduate from high school. I'm going to be a pilot just like you."

"You're Joey, right?"

"Yes sir."

"Well Joey, the Air Force wants men with at least two years of college for pilot training. Wait until you're qualified, then give it a go."

"The family doesn't have money for college."

"I heard your grades are pretty good, Joey. Talk to Steve's wife about scholarships. I need to get back to my wife. Don't mess with my airplane…Okay?"

"Yes sir."

Back in the kitchen, Peggy was smearing icing on the on the steaming roll with a vengeance. She turned to Tommy. "Tell me the whole story on these assignments you have and why you have them. I thought you were going to be a fighter pilot when they recalled you."

"I'll be flying fighters with the Korean air force as an instructor. I'll be there for six months and then back to Scott Field. The choices I was given accept this assignment or be the Officer's Club manager. I'll be back in time for the baby's arrival. I promise."

"Somehow that promise sounds pretty hollow to me. Damn it, Tommy. Why can't you stay with me? I want you to chew on this while you're away. If you're not here when the baby arrives, I'm going to box your ears. Do you understand me? Never mind answering that, just hold me… but first who are they?"

"Peggy, I really don't know."

DEDICATION

Christmas Help is respectfully dedicated to all who served in our nation's two World Wars. They are the recipients of this nation's Victory Medal, an award that has eluded this country's warriors since those events.

Permission to include Margaret Rorke's poem entitled "Love" in *Christmas Help* was granted By Margaret Curry Rorke's (1915-2000) daughter Margaret Ann Rorke, Associate Professor of Musicology, University of Utah, September 14, 2008.

I would like to thank the members of the Dallas Fort Worth Writers' Workshop and Carmen Goldthwaite's Writers' Circle for their help and encouragement in keeping my story on track.

A quick summary of my military career: Enlisted in Marine Corps Reserve in 1948 and served for almost two years. Enlisted in USAF January 1951. Entered the aviation cadet program in August 1952 and received

Tony Skur

my pilot's wings and commission in September/October 1953. I served in six fighter squadrons, flying the F86-D, F101 and A-1 Sky Raiders in Southeast Asia. I commanded an Air Defense Group, then became Regional Director of Weapon Controllers. My last assignment was Deputy Commander Operations for the 20th Air Division. I accumulated over 5,000 hours of flying time in jet fighters/trainers and prop fighters.

Graduated from Mount Saint Marys in Emmitsburg, Maryland with a BS in Business and Finance. I received a Masters in Liberal Arts from Texas Christian University, Fort Worth, Texas.

TO BE RELEASED IN DECEMBER

More to Come...Tommy's Air force career is interrupted by his CIA contact, who enrolls him in the Army's intelligence course and Jump school at Fort Benning, Georgia. These adventures have unforeseen consequences on his marriage and disastrous results on his officer efficiency reports.

One more Time...Thompson is tapped by his CIA memes to ferry Corsair fighters to the French during the siege at Dein Bein Phu. He selects his World War Two buddy as his wingman, but ends up leading his friend's wife Tina to more combat missions than he bargained for. Did I mention temptations?

IN THE WORKS

New story...Peter, the Green Beret son of Tina Jackson, helps in rescuing American POW's from a Laotian jungle prison camp. His mother presents him with her "no die Buddha" as he becomes the go to man for his CIA handler. His biggest problem is, he falls in love, or is it lust, with a beautiful Air Force nurse, Ginger, and an intelligence officer Gloria. Many twists and turns as he tries to investigate the drug trade in Southeast Asia.

CPSIA information can be obtained at www.ICGtesting.com
Printed in the USA
LVOW06s1619081113

360532LV00002B/14/P